Worth The Price

Now. It had to be now or she would lose her nerve. Let the glow of the wine and the good vibes she was feeling from Twain be her guide and get it over with. If he said no, it was better to know that now so she didn't waste any more time.

She put her knitting back down and turned quickly, Twain's gaze coming up from her ass to her eyes just as quickly.

A grin crossed his face, rough and manly with a three-day growth. A grin that said "Busted" but also that he didn't care.

"Twain, I need to ask you something."

"Okay," he said, still grinning. Until he noticed her rubbing her hands on her hips, a habit she had when she was nervous. The grin gone, he leaned forward on the edge of the bed, almost touching her. "Liv?" he said.

"It's more of a favor really," she said, swallowing hard. As much wine as she'd drunk, you wouldn't think her mouth could go this dry.

He reached out, his long arms touching her. He rested a hand on each of hers, stilling their nervous movement. "Anything, Liv. You know that."

Yes, he'd done anything and everything she'd asked of him. When they were married and after.

Except for one thing.

But this wasn't about that. It wasn't even really about Twain.

This was for her. And she deserved to have it.

She took a step toward him, his hands staying on her hips even as she took hers and placed them on his shoulders.

"Twain," she said, bolstering herself with a deep breath. "I want another baby."

With the look of shock and confusion just beginning on his face, she added the kicker.

"And I want it to be yours."

OTHER TITLES BY
MARA JACOBS

WORTH the PRICE

The Worth Series, Book Five

MARA JACOBS

Published by Mara Jacobs
©Copyright 2015 Mara Jacobs

ISBN: 978-1-940993-02-7

For more information on the author and her works, please see www.marajacobs.com

For My Other Kelly

Prologue

Sixteen Years Ago

LIV KOSKELA SAT IN HER AGES-OLD CHEVY CAVALIER, waiting until her boyfriend, Twain Beck, came out of his dorm to join her. The heater was turned full blast, but January in the Copper Country demanded more than she could coax from the old engine, and she rubbed her mittened hands together for added warmth. Or perhaps out of nervousness. Most likely both.

The worn leather of her brother Joe's choppers rasped loudly from the friction. Ugly as sin, the battered mittens were the warmest she'd found. She thought how nice it would be to have something as warm as the work gloves, but cute, young, and feminine.

Yes, think about mittens. That would keep her mind off what was about to happen with Twain.

Her grandmother used to knit before her hands had become gnarled from severe arthritis. Maybe she could teach Liv how to make cute mittens that were also really warm. Warm enough to wait in cold ice arenas, freezing cars, and outside Tech dorms while her boyfriend of eight months finished up whatever he was doing. Without her.

Twain had always been the life of the party, even back at Calumet High School, where they'd both graduated last year. Funny, gregarious, so likeable.

It was one reason she'd always been so attracted to him. That and his big, strong hockey defenseman body. And his almost-black hair, worn a little longer in the back. And those green, green eyes.

In the spring of their senior year, they'd somehow found themselves alone in the kitchen at a house party of one of their classmates. They'd both been a little drunk, which worked in Liv's favor, because otherwise she would have been way too nervous to respond to Twain's halfhearted flirtations.

And they had been halfhearted. Liv didn't fool herself on that. Two months prior, Twain had broken up with Jenny Korpii, his girlfriend of two years. And though Liv knew of a few hookups since then, it appeared that Twain was still licking his Jenny wounds and wasn't looking for a girlfriend. It was commonly felt that it was just a matter of time before Twain and Jenny got back together.

He'd be going to Tech to play hockey in the fall, and even though Houghton was only a twenty-minute drive down US 41 from Calumet, it was another world from their little cocoon up north.

At least it was to Liv and her family, who, after graduating from high school, had all stayed in Calumet to raise their families and work at the family restaurant, Koskela's Kitchen.

But that night in Paula Ilonen's kitchen, Twain Beck had flirted with Liv out of what seemed more like someone trying to practice rusty skills than making any real romantic overture.

And Liv had drunk just enough to come out of her shell and return Twain's serve, shaky as it was.

She'd had the hand-me-down Cavalier that night, the same one she sat in now, and they'd driven to the Calumet Water Works park and hastily—and awkwardly—had sex in the back seat. A not-so-small feat, given Twain's size.

It had been Liv's first time, though obviously not Twain's. He'd led her through it all, showing her how and where. Though she hadn't experienced an orgasm, she'd thrilled with the sensations

Twain gave her.

She'd been happy he'd chosen her to go home with, but hadn't kidded herself that it would be anything more than that one night. She was happy to have that much of him. Until he'd called her the next day and asked her out.

And that very day the fear started in Liv that had only escalated over the past eight months.

When would she lose Twain Beck?

She'd been fully prepared—though filled with dread—after graduation, figuring Twain would want to spend the summer with his buddies before going in different directions in the fall for various colleges and full-time jobs.

But he had continued to call, to make plans, and to spend most evenings with Liv, driving around in her car (Twain's mother only had one car and needed it most of the time), going to the beach, heading down to Lake Linden for ice cream, and, of course, making out.

When he started Tech, made new friends, and began practicing with the hockey team, Liv became a puddle of nerves, waiting for "the talk" from Twain, or to not hear anything from him at all.

Although he could have easily commuted from Calumet to campus, his scholarship included room and board, so he'd moved into Co-Ed Hall. The name alone filled Liv with images of nubile female freshmen walking through the hallways with towels barely covering said nubile bodies.

She didn't blame him. She was dying to get out from under her parents' roof too, although she got along well with them. With four older siblings already gone, it was just Liv and her younger brother Joe still at home.

But two days after moving into the dorm, Twain had called and asked her to join him at a Tech hockey party. The knot in her stomach eased an infinitesimal amount.

The knot—so identifiable, she'd come to think of it as her Pet Rock—had stayed with her throughout the fall as Twain made new friends and she worked in the family restaurant while taking a course for administrative assistants through Gogebic Community College. She didn't have a lot of local prospects and had never been a great student, but she was determined not to smell like pasties every night when she came home.

They were together a few nights of the week and on the weekends when they were able given his classes and hockey schedule and her life, such as it was. Revolving around Twain and his schedule was something Liv did gladly, though he'd never asked her to. Somewhere deep inside of her, she knew that she was selling herself short. But she also knew that having familiar, energetic sex with Twain whenever he wanted would help her keep him.

And that was what her world boiled down to. Keeping him happy. Not giving him any reason to look elsewhere for female companionship.

Now, Liv watched as Twain exited the dorm and made his way up the snow-covered steps to the road that ran behind the dorms. Liv watched Twain walk with a strong confidence, his large body stepping with certainty, even on a likely icy walkway.

Once again, Liv wondered if today was the day she would lose Twain forever. He would be twenty soon. She'd had a crush on him since sixth grade and had been in love with him since the night of Paula Ilonen's party.

But after what she had to tell him tonight…

"Hey," he said, sliding into the passenger seat and leaning across to give her a soft kiss on the cheek.

"Hey," she whispered. Then, afraid that in a half-hour she would never again get the chance to kiss his mouth, she leaned closer to him, grabbed his coat with her leather choppers, and pulled him toward her. Kissing him was easy, had always been easy. And the sex, after that first half-drunken time, had become wonderful and soul satisfying to Liv.

But kissing Twain Beck was what Liv Koskela loved more than anything in the world.

He picked up quickly, taking the lead from her, melding his lips to hers, sweeping his warm tongue into her mouth.

She gasped, as she always did, and he kissed her more deeply. Clinging to him, she never wanted the kiss to stop, but he eventually pulled back and chuckled as he said, "I've missed you too, Liv." His green eyes sparkled in the light that shone through her windshield.

Liv burst into tears.

"Jesus, Liv. What is it?" He started patting her arms, like he was frisking her. "Are you hurt? What is it?"

Of course, Twain would automatically think something was wrong with her physically. She'd been very—*very*—careful to hide her true feelings from him. To mask the depth of her love for a man who was happy to just take things as they came. In life and in love.

"I'm…fine. I'm…okay," she said through gulps of trying to make the sobs stop. She did not want to cry during this. Not if this was the last time she would be in Twain's arms with that gentle, concerned look on his face as he gazed at her.

"Okay, take a breath," he said, rubbing a hand up and down her thick down coat, no longer checking for breaks, though his motions of comfort were startlingly similar. "It's okay. It'll be okay. I'm here now."

That last part Liv hung on to like a life raft. Yes, he was here now. And she wasn't *certain* that he would leave her.

She pulled herself together, looked into those beautiful eyes, and said, "Twain, I'm pregnant."

His hand didn't drop from her arm, which she took as a good sign. Nor did he turn away from her. But he was silent for a very long time. Liv didn't say a word. Later, she didn't want him to remember her leading him in any particular direction. She had that much sense about her even though she was nineteen, pregnant, and a waitress at her family's restaurant.

She wasn't sure how much time had passed before he started nodding and a slow smile spread across his face. For just a moment, her Pet Rock faded into the background.

"Liv," he said, looking her in the eye. He cleared his throat and began again. "Olivia Koskela, will you marry me?"

A rush of relief ran through her, and a huge sigh expelled from her body, rushing out as she hugged him, saying, "Yes, yes," over and over.

He murmured words of comfort, promising a bright future, one that he would be a part of. "I'll take care of you, Liv. I swear I will."

And somewhere, deep inside, the same question she woke up with every morning insinuated itself even deeper into Liv's psyche.

When would she lose Twain Beck?

One

TWAIN BECK STEPPED INTO THE CAT'S MEOW, SAW PETEY
Ryan and Zeke Hampton at the bar, and almost walked back out.

It wasn't that he disliked either of the guys. Hell, he wasn't
even sure the last time he'd seen them both. Oh yeah, he'd seen
Petey at Katie Maki's wedding last fall. Had Zeke been there too?
Home on leave? That night had been pretty much a blur to him.

Twain started to turn to leave, but just then, Petey raised his
head and caught Twain's eye.

"Hey, Becks, how ya doing?" Petey said, loudly enough that
the few other people in the bar raised their heads and looked
toward Twain. "Join us."

Twain nodded and made his way to the far end of the bar.
He didn't come to the Cat's Meow often, preferring Tootie's in
his nearby hometown of Calumet when he wanted a beer. But his
son Matt lived in Houghton with Twain's ex-wife, Liv, so he often
found himself in the area of the Cat's Meow after having dinner
with Matt and dropping him off. Or when he'd finished up a job
on this side of the lift bridge. Most times, he drove past, went
through Hancock, and made his way to his house in Calumet.
But tonight he felt like a beer.

"Good to see you," Petey said, slapping a heavy hand on
Twain's shoulder. "Been a while."

Twain nodded, acknowledging Petey's words, and then
moved to Zeke, who was standing up to greet Twain.

8 ❦ MARA JACOBS

"Hey, man," Zeke said, extending his hand and then clasping an arm around Twain as they shook. Twain returned the bro hug. "How ya been?" the Navy pilot asked.

"Been good, thanks. How 'bout you? You out, or just on leave?"

Petey grunted a laugh. "Out? Zeke's never getting out. He's a lifer, for sure."

The look of uncertainty in Zeke's eye as Twain moved away from him told a different story, but Twain let it lie. He saw Zeke Hampton *maybe* every couple of years, and only for brief moments like this. It wasn't Twain's business if Zeke was having a career crisis.

"On a quick leave," Zeke answered Twain, ignoring Petey. "Home to see my nephew." Then, as an afterthought, he added, "And my family."

Twain remembered those first precious months of Matt's life. How it seemed as though every night when Twain came home from a day of classes and then hockey practice, Matt had seemed to grow an inch and learned to do something new.

Zeke was just an uncle to baby Sam Robbins, but Sam's mother, Lizzie Robbins, was Zeke's twin, so there was probably a deeper bond to the kid for Zeke.

"He's got to be, what, four or five months now?" Twain asked. He vividly remembered Lizzie going into labor at Katie Maki's wedding, but he couldn't quite recall exactly when that had been.

"Just hit six months," Zeke said.

Twain nodded and motioned to the bartender that he'd have the same draft beer that his friends were having, and then sat on a stool on the other side of Zeke. "Goes by fast," Twain said.

Both men nodded. Zeke asked, "How's Matty? He's got to be…what? Thirteen, fourteen by now?"

"Fifteen. Sixteen next fall," Twain answered, feeling decades older than the two men he sat with, even though they were the same age.

The three of them had been really close at Tech when they were freshman. Twain and Petey because both of them were on the hockey team, and Petey and Zeke because Petey had dated Lizzie for a short time before they had ended up being best friends.

Lizzie and her two best friends had gone to State, and Petey and Zeke had become tight, including Twain in their little group.

They'd been tight, and if Twain hadn't had two brothers, he would have had Zeke and Petey stand up for him when he and Liv got married in the spring of freshman year. But they were keeping the wedding small, just family and close friends, so Twain had chosen to have his brothers, Sawyer and Huck, stand with him.

Probably just as well, since Twain had to drop out of Tech midway through his second year. After that, he'd slowly drifted away from his Tech friends, including Petey and Zeke.

"Fifteen?" Petey said, sounding as shocked as Twain often felt when he thought about the passing of the years. "Holy shit, where did that go?"

"Well, for you, it went to the NHL," Twain said. He took a drink of his beer, liking how the handle of the big mug felt in his hands. "And for you"—he nodded in Zeke's direction—"it went to the US Navy."

He tried to listen to how his voice sounded. Was there bitterness? Contempt? Or—and this thought really pissed him off—self-pity?

He didn't think so. In fact, he sounded proud and happy for his former buddies (*current* buddies, he would classify, if pressed). Both had achieved exactly what they'd wanted all those years ago when they would hang in his dorm room and talk about the future.

His dream and Petey's had been the same—to play in the NHL. Zeke wanted to fly fighter jets.

Two out of three ain't bad.

"He's doing great," Twain said, pulling himself out of the past. He'd come to terms long ago with the path his life had taken. *Matty.* "He won't let me call him Matty anymore—strictly Matt.

His hair is too long, and he's skiing instead of playing hockey. But he's..." Damn, his voice cracked and his throat was closing up thinking about how much he loved his son. And around these two guys? Shit, he was going to take some heat for that.

Zeke gave him a good-natured punch in the arm. "We get it. He's...yours."

Twain nodded, giving Zeke a thankful glance and then taking a good, long swallow of beer.

Maybe they had all grown up from the shit-talking, ball-busting college freshmen they'd been when they'd first become friends.

"Skiing?" Petey cried. "Instead of hockey? What kind of kid are you raising?"

Or maybe they'd just gotten older and not grown up.

"I'm just yanking your chain," Petey explained. "Good for him. Skiing he can do forever. Especially up here."

That was definitely true. Even in early March, there were a few weeks left to Matt's ski season, with the U.P. finals in Marquette not far off. Some years, Matt was able to ski well into April.

The Copper Country, the northwestern tip of Michigan's Upper Peninsula, had record amounts of snowfall due to being at the shores of Lake Superior. A paradise if your kid wanted nothing more than to ski and snowboard.

But sometimes a detriment to your business if you were a logger. The short days in the winter and the major thaws in the spring causing the ground to be too soft for large equipment could make things challenging.

"Speaking of hockey," Twain said to Petey, "I was sorry to hear about your knee."

Petey tipped his mug of beer toward Twain in acknowledgement, then took a drink. When he placed his mug back on the bar, he slapped his knee. "Good as new, now."

"And yet you retired?" Twain asked. He would have thought Petey Ryan would need to be dragged off the ice because he loved the game so much.

"It was time," Petey said. Twain was just about to question him further when Petey added, "Chapter Two in the Life and Times of Petey Ryan has begun."

Twain let out a small snort of laughter. Petey always had been pretty full of himself, but in a "Yeah, I know it's all bullshit" kind of way that people found endearing.

And by people, Twain meant women.

"Yeah? That's great, I guess," Twain said, not quite believing his words.

"It is great," Petey said. "My knee is good. I got out before I had too many concussions," At this, he knocked the wooden bar made of a beautiful polished ash that Twain had always admired. "I've got a new business venture going." Twain opened his mouth to question Petey on that, but his former defensive lineman kept on going, "And…I am crazy in love." He raised his glass, and Zeke and Twain automatically raised theirs to clink them together.

"To being in love," Zeke said at the same time Twain said, "To your new business venture."

The three men looked at each other, laughed, and then took hearty swigs from their mugs.

"Cold, Becks, very cold," Petey said as they all set their mugs back on the bar. "Out of all that, business trumps love?"

"Sorry, man. But business ventures are something new for you, right?"

"Ouch," Zeke said, laughing at Twain's jab.

"Hey, I'll have you know," Petey said to Twain, while shooting Zeke a "Shut the hell up" look, "that I have only been in love like this once before. And…it was with the same girl."

"Seriously?" both Zeke and Twain said. "When 'before'?" Zeke asked, while Twain said, "Who is she?"

"Alison Jukuri," Petey answered Twain. It was obvious that this wasn't news to Zeke, but the fact that it wasn't the first time was. He seemed to be scouring the past, trying to bring to mind Petey and Alison over the years.

Twain couldn't ever remember them hooking up in the past

either. In fact, in the few times he'd been around them both, it seemed Alison thoroughly enjoyed dressing Petey down. But then, Twain had pretty much been out of the loop of their lives since Tech. Oh, he'd see Petey around during the summers here and there and would be invited to weddings and such, but after dropping out of Tech, Twain had pretty much committed himself to Liv and Matt.

Until he'd fucked that up.

Flashes of clothes thrown all across the bedroom floor, of bodies in bed, and of Liv's look of complete devastation ran through his mind, but he tried to push the memory aside.

"Congrats," Twain said. "Really, that's great." He gave a salute with his mug and downed the rest of his beer.

He'd been tremendously envious of Petey's NHL career, in part because they'd been on the same line together and Twain felt he could play as well as Petey. At least during their first two years at Tech.

There had always been a giant "what if" about hockey that had hung over Twain's head all these years that was personified in Petey Ryan. But Twain had taken solace in the fact that he had a great woman who loved him and a wonderful kid in Matty.

And though he was truly happy his old friend had fallen in love (apparently again) with a good person, it brought out those old feelings of restlessness, and a twinge of jealousy, in Twain.

Which was ridiculous. He loved being a logger. His love for his son was bone deep and so raw it almost hurt at times.

But he didn't have a woman who loved him.

He didn't have Liv.

"When did you and Al—" Zeke started, but Petey cut his friend off.

"Actually, speaking of my new business venture, your brother Sawyer was a big help. I just signed up Summers and Beck to build it."

"Yeah?" Twain asked. Good. That was good. Talk about business and Sawyer and stuff like that. Definitely not about love and the fact that Petey looked happier than Twain had ever seen him, while Twain looked… He took a glance at himself in the mirror, which ran the length of the room behind the bar. Tired. He looked tired.

"What is the firm building for you?"

"An indoor driving range. I've got some land up by the airport that we're going to use."

Again, the news was something Zeke had obviously heard before, and he started eyeing up the table of women who had come in after Twain.

"Really?" Twain said, thinking about it. "I don't golf, so I wouldn't know, but I'm guessing there'd be a big market for that up here."

"That's what we're counting on. I'm doing it with Darío Luna, the guy Katie married."

Twain nodded. "They just had a kid, right?"

Petey nodded. "Yep. Girl. Peaches."

"Peaches? Peaches Luna?"

Both Zeke and Petey snorted. "I know, I know. I guess it had some meaning for them. It's not her real name, but it's the only thing they call her," Petey said, then looked at Zeke. "What *is* her real name, anyway?"

Zeke stared off into space, then shrugged. "I don't know. I'm sure Lizzie told me, but…"

They all shrugged it off as not important, though Twain bet that it was sure important to Katie and Darío.

"And you hired Summers and Beck to do it for you?" Twain said, remembering a big project that his friend Deni had worked on just before he met her.

"We did. Your brother and Deni Casparich are the points on it. Looks like they've got something going on."

Twain nodded. It was impossible to be around Deni and Sawyer and not see their connection. Both total engineering geeks, their minds were totally in sync, and their chemistry was off the charts. Sawyer had almost blown it with Deni, but Twain had helped him get his head out of his ass and recognize that Deni was the best thing that had ever happened to him.

Twain still felt protective of Deni, even though the sunny days of March had done great things for her situation. He tried to meet her at least once a week, whether Sawyer could make it or not.

He hadn't seen a ton of his brother in the month since Sawyer and Deni made up, but he had gone out to lunch and dinner with Deni quite a bit. She and Twain had bonded when she'd had a bad episode of her seasonal affective disorder and Sawyer had been too much of a chickenshit to deal with it.

"Yep. Seems like everyone's in love," Twain said. He and Petey looked to Zeke, who laughed.

"Oh, hell no. I am *not* about to become a besotted fool like Petey, here. Or Sawyer, it seems."

"That is definitely the way to describe Sawyer these days," Twain said. He was happy for his brother, who had found love again after losing his wife, Molly, in a car accident ten years ago. But again, that twinge of envy crept over Twain.

It had been a weird day. First, he'd had to walk the land of a prospective client on snowshoes, leaving him exhausted. Then he'd had dinner with Matt after picking him up at the ski hill. Which had been good and normal. But then when he'd dropped Matt off, Liv had asked him to come in to talk about the upcoming ski team schedule.

Totally normal stuff that as co-parents they did all the time. After they had their schedules set, she'd seemed like she was trying to work up to asking or telling him something, but she never did. Something about sitting at the bar of Liv's kitchen, her single plate from eating alone left at the side of the sink, waiting for her to talk to him, and not being able to, had enveloped Twain in a sadness that he could neither understand nor deny.

Thus the stop at the Cat's Meow.

"In fact," Zeke said, rising and grabbing his mug, "I am so committed to not falling in love that I'm off to pursue other—

short-term—arrangements." He walked over to the table of women. Seconds later, he was sitting with them, saying something that made all three of them giggle.

"Probably making them wet with his war-hero stories," Petey said, watching his friend.

"Says the pro hockey player, who, of course, never used that as an opening with women."

Petey laughed, and the sound reminded Twain of all the good times they'd had at Tech while Twain had been a part of the team.

Not wanting the sadness of earlier, and the envy of the past few minutes, to pull him under, he tried to bring the conversation back to safer ground.

"So, when's your driving range going to open? Didn't make it for this winter, eh?"

Petey shook his head. "Nah. Didn't even have the idea until I was recuperating from the knee surgery. Sawyer and his crew worked fast to get the specs and bid done, and Darío and I signed off a few weeks ago, but they can't even break ground until the snow's gone. Probably won't be complete until September. People will be on the real driving ranges then, but we'll get 'em when it turns cold."

"Which could very well be September," Twain added, and Petey nodded in agreement.

"Actually, I was thinking of calling you when we got closer," Petey said.

"Yeah?"

"We're going to try to get a liquor license for the place. We're not going to get rich on a bucket of balls—and that's not why we're doing it—but it would be great to keep people there after they're done hitting. Have a beer or two. Might make people come in a pair or group instead of just one person coming to hit a quick bucket."

"Yeah, that makes sense."

"Maybe even do pizzas or burgers. We're still working out the ROI on that, but— What?"

Twain was shaking his head. "Nothing. It's just I never thought I'd hear you throw out terms like ROI."

"It means return on investment."

"I know what it means. I'm just surprised you do."

"Fuck you, Becks," Petey said good-naturedly. He took a sip of beer, then looked back at Twain with his trademark shit-eating grin. "I just learned it a month ago."

Twain laughed long and loud, causing the table of women to look over at Petey and him, some with definite interest. Which then caused Zeke to give them both a "Don't cock-block me, bro" look.

Both Twain and Petey were large men. Like NHL defensemen large. Both had dark hair and were kind of craggy and well worn. And they'd both had their share of female appreciation over the years, though Petey, given his occupation and traveling, had been able to take better advantage of that.

Though not as big and rough as Petey and Twain, Zeke Hampton was a flyboy, a war hero, and had the good looks and swagger that went with it. Twain had no worries that Zeke would be able to leave with any of the three women.

Hell, maybe all three.

"Anyway," Petey continued, covertly flipping a bird at Zeke. "If we get the license, I was thinking of a really nice wood bar." He rubbed his hand along the bar at which they sat, his huge fingers stroking with the grain. "But circular and made out of…I don't know. That's why I was going to call you."

"To ask which wood?"

"Well, that. But also to ask if you wanted to build it for us."

"I don't do a lot of custom work anymore," Twain said, but in a voice that left the door open.

"Because you don't like it or don't have time for it?"

"No time. I bought Eddie out. I'm running the business now."

Petey nodded in understanding. "Congrats. Well, if we know the specs now, you'd have a lot of lead time to work on it."

"I could just tell you a couple kinds of wood that would look best and give you some names of guys who could do the work for you."

"Yeah, thanks. If that's as far as you want to be involved in it, that's cool." The large man shifted in his seat. "See, here's the deal. The place is basically a big, ugly balloon. There's no way around that. But if we had an area that was, I don't know…warmer, more inviting than just steel beams and parachute material, I think people would stick around longer."

"Yeah, you're right."

"And I want it to be good. I want it to be Beck-brother good."

"Well, you've already got one Beck brother working on that for you."

Petey grinned. "You know me, Becks. I'm a greedy bastard. I want you both."

Twain liked the sensation of being in demand. He had been years ago for his custom-made wood pieces, but he made more money in straight logging, so had shifted his time to that almost exclusively. Then he had become partners with Eddie and was now running the business completely on his own.

"You know I'm going to hound you about this. Might as well say yes now," Petey said.

Twain laughed again and drained his beer. "Okay. Yes. Deni and Sawyer can get me the specs?"

Petey, unable to disguise his smile of triumph, just nodded.

"I'll start thinking about woods."

"Shit, I think about wood all the time," Petey said.

"You do know we're in our mid-thirties, right? No longer in middle school?"

Petey just flashed him another smile. As Twain reached for his wallet, Petey stopped him. "It's on me. Turned out to be a business meeting."

Twain didn't fight him, but made a mental note to treat the next time he saw Petey. He didn't have NHL money, and having a kid who skied was plenty expensive, but he was no charity case.

Twain raised a hand to Zeke, who returned his wave. "See ya next time in town," Zeke said.

"Keep your head down in that jet," Twain said. "No easy target."

Zeke gave him a look of indignation. "Shit, ain't no one going to get me when I'm in my bird."

Twain guessed that was more for the ladies' benefit, so he just smiled at his old friend. He turned to leave, but Petey reached out and grabbed his arm.

"It was really good to see you, Becks. I thought about you a lot when I was playing. I never did have as good a defensive linemate as I did with you."

Twain gave a small smile. "We were a good team."

"That we were. You know, I always really admired you. Marrying Liv, quitting school, not only raising Matt, but being a really good dad."

Petey hadn't been around much after Matty had turned two, but even then, it was obvious how much Twain loved his son. It had been an easy decision to leave school and the all-encompassing life of collegiate hockey to be able to support and spend time with his family.

"Thanks, man. It's what anyone would have done in my situation."

Petey shook his head. "No. No, I don't think it is. There was a time… I mean, I almost had to… Our lives were kind of similar…" Twain waited for Petey. The guy was obviously trying to say something meaningful, but held back.

"I thought about you a lot. And how, if things had been a tiny bit different, it could have been me."

Twain guessed every guy on the team had thought that when he'd gotten Liv pregnant. And then made sure they were doubly protected with their girlfriends.

But there was something in Petey's voice…

"Anyway," he finally said. "Just wanted you to know I was thinking of you, and I think you handled yourself well back then."

"Thanks, man."

"I mean it. And you guys gave it a good run. Eight years you were married?"

Twain only nodded.

"Man, I would have fucked it up *way* before you did. I probably wouldn't have lasted that long."

Twain bristled at the unintended dig. He'd heard it all, and not usually in any admiring way.

Usually he'd been called "cheating dickhead" by the people who felt they were in the know.

But there was no judgment in Petey's voice. Just understanding and perhaps a bit of relief. As he always did when people brought up his past, Twain swallowed down a response.

"Although you never know, do you?"

"Nope, you never know," Twain said, wondering now if Petey was still talking about Twain and Liv, or perhaps himself and... Would it have been Alison? Even way back then?

No. They had shared shit like that at the time.

Suddenly wearier than he'd been after he'd walked Toivo Juntunen's property earlier in the day, Twain placed a hand on Petey's shoulder, gave a squeeze, and said, "Keep in touch about the bar."

He heard Petey say he would as Twain walked out of the bar and into the snowy night.

Two

—∞—

AS LIV BECK WALKED INTO THE COMMODORE TO PICK up her son, she pulled her phone out of her bag and realized it had been on silent since she'd sat in on the dean's three o'clock meeting.

Practice ran long. Going to be more like 7 by the time we're done.

Shoot. No wonder Matt hadn't been waiting in the vestibule when she drove up.

She'd been ticked that she'd had to park and get out of her warm car to go into the Commodore to get him, but apparently that was on her, as Twain had given her plenty of notice.

Quickly debating turning around and going back to her office on the Tech campus to get some more work done, waiting in the car, or running to the grocery store, Liv heard, "Hey, Mom," from across the restaurant.

Matty came out of the men's room in the main room and stood waiting at the ramp that led to the larger room, which looked out onto the lake.

She didn't want to venture that far because then Twain would be able to see her if he was facing in the right direction. But Matty didn't move, waiting for her. Reluctantly, she made her way to her son, stopping at the base of the ramp, keeping her back to the other room.

"I just saw your father's text," she said. "So I'm going to go back to the office. Text me—"

"Liv," Twain's deep voice said from behind her. Seven years divorced and that damn voice still sent a shiver through her. Turning around, she repeated to Twain that she'd just seen his text. "Matty's—"

"Matt," her son interrupted her.

"*Matt's* going to text me when you're finished."

"Did you just come from work?" Twain asked her. She nodded. "Then join us. You've got to be as starved as we are."

"Oh, no, I don't want to intrude on your time together."

"It's fine. We ordered enough for an army." He watched as a heavily laden waitress came out of the kitchen with two large trays. "In fact, looks like we're just about to be served. Really. Join us." He reached out a hand and touched her on the arm. His green eyes had always done her in, and his touch, even through the layers of her down parka and sweater, seemed to warm her in a way that the car heater hadn't.

"Okay. I am hungry. Thanks," she said. Twain stepped aside to allow her to go first. When she got into the room, the waitress had gone to a table where a young woman—probably a Tech student—sat, making room for the three pizzas the waitress was unloading.

"Guess that wasn't your food," Liv said to Matt, who was walking by her side. But even as she said it, she knew she was wrong. There were no other tables in the area that had people seated at them, jackets slung over chairs, or drink glasses. And the table with the woman had two seats that were obviously previously occupied. Matty's jacket on the back of one confirmed her worst fears.

Twain was dating a much younger woman—a girl, really. And it was probably semi-serious if he was bringing her around Matty, something he didn't do.

"No, that's ours," Matty said, taking his seat next to the woman who was now rising from hers and smiling at Liv.

Not waiting for introductions, her son scooped several slices of pizza onto his plate and started inhaling the food.

"Slow down," Liv and Twain said at the same time. She looked over her shoulder at Twain and they smiled at each other with looks of parental resignation. Twain even rolled his eyes and shrugged his shoulders at Matty's inability to take anything less than entire mouthfuls at a time.

"Well, there's co-parenting at its most unified," said the woman as she held out her hand to Liv. "Deni Casparich. You must be Liv."

With a closer look, the woman was definitely older than a Tech student. But still quite a bit younger than Liv and Twain's thirty-five. She was dressed in jeans and a black turtleneck with an unbuttoned gray cardigan. Her thick chestnut hair was pulled back in a ponytail, and she wore little makeup, if any. Very girl next door.

Liv wanted to hate her on sight, but Deni's smile was warm and Liv found herself smiling back as she shook Deni's hand.

"Yes," Liv said. "Liv Beck. I don't mean to intrude on your dinner."

Deni waved Liv's apology away as she sat back down in her chair. "Not interrupting at all. But you better sit down and start eating, or Matt is going to leave us nothing but pizza crusts."

"Hey," Matty said with feigned hurt, looking at Deni. She raised a brow at him and then they both started laughing. "Yeah, Mom, she's probably right. Dig in."

Ever the gentleman, Twain held her coat for her as she slipped out of it and then placed it on the back of her chair as she sat down.

"Wine?" Twain asked her as he motioned to the waitress.

"Please."

"A glass of Cab," he told the waitress as she approached. A quick nod and she spun back toward the bar. Twain then sat down next to Liv, Deni on his other side.

It seemed so familiar for Twain to be ordering her type of wine and to be having pizza at the Commodore with the two men in her life.

But it had been years since they'd done that. And Twain was no longer a man in her life.

The sad part was that between pick-ups and drop-offs, seeing each other at Matty's events, and phone calls about scheduling, Twain was the man she spent the most time with these days, other than those at the office.

But apparently the reverse was not true, if Deni's obvious ease with Twain and Matty was any indication.

A wave of despair washed over her. This new development did not work well with the plans she'd been fostering.

"How was practice?" she asked Matty as the waitress set down a healthy glass of red wine in front of her. Liv, needing a good bolstering, took a deep swallow.

"Good. Really good," he said, not looking up from his pizza to Liv. Then he did take his eyes away from his next bite to look up. But not at Liv. "Can you come to my next meet?" he asked Deni.

"When is it?" Deni said while Liv took another drink from her wine, her throat suddenly very dry.

"Thursday. Right after school. At Mont Ripley. You could even walk there from your house."

"Oh, sorry. I'm going to be in Marquette Thursday checking out a possible project. It's the only day the owner of the building will be in town." At the look of disappointment in Matty's eyes (a look that still crushed Liv, even though she'd learned to hide it when Matty was little), Deni added, "Rain check. I will get to the one after. Promise."

Matty nodded and returned to his pizza, satisfied with Deni's answer. Something he'd said finally hit Liv—Matty knew where Deni lived. Had he spent the night there when Twain had him?

Liv didn't think so. Over the years, when one of them would be in a relationship, they were very careful to make sure that Matty was with the other if there were…overnight guests.

A couple years after the divorce, when things had become friendlier and hatchets had been buried—or at least placed on the ground for the time being—they'd discussed exposing Matty to significant others. They'd decided on a four-month rule. If either of them had been seeing someone for over four months, they would tell the other and then sit down with Matty and talk about it before bringing the new person into their son's life.

She'd had that talk with Twain only once. He'd never had it with her.

And still hadn't, even though she was sitting across from Deni, watching as the young woman took another slice of sausage pizza.

Maybe Liv had nothing to worry about. Not that she worried about Twain finding someone, of course. Her concern was only for her son. Well, Matty wasn't her *only* concern. But it was starting to look like she'd need to do some more thinking about her other big concern.

She took a deep breath and then another long drink of wine, trying to call up her internal gauge of Twain Pain.

The barometer had been low for the past few years, only pinging ever so slightly when she'd see him during one of Matty's events.

Now, the meter seemed to be skittering higher and higher. She tried to be cool, set her wine glass down, and took some of the tostada pizza.

"So, where did you two meet?" she asked Twain and Deni, not really looking at either.

"Twain was… We were… I was…" Deni's stuttering made Liv look up from her plate to see the young woman's eyes locked on Twain and her face quickly turning beet red.

Liv glanced at Twain at her side to see the same look of embarrassment as Deni. Then they smiled at each other, and Liv's Twain Pain meter skyrocketed.

"Deni works at Summers and Beck," Twain finally said, still not taking his eyes from Deni.

They came to some kind of silent collusion. Deni gave just the tiniest nod of agreement—and thanks?—to Twain before turning to Liv and nodding. "Yes. I work at Sawyer's firm."

She was hiding something about how she and Twain met, but Liv let it go. Probably best not to know, even though "what-ifs" had been her worst enemy over the years. Sometimes imagination could be a real bitch.

Then it registered with Liv that for the firm to be the connection (or at least the one they were admitting to) for Twain and Deni… "Is Sawyer back at the firm?" she asked Twain.

He looked at Deni again and smiled. Then he turned his attention to Liv. "Yep. About a month now. Going into the office and everything."

Involuntarily, she laid a hand on Twain's arm, the heat of the strong man coming through the wool of his sweater. "Oh, Twain. That's wonderful."

He looked down at her hand on his arm, and she quickly pulled it back, embarrassed. A quick glance at Deni confirmed that she'd seen the contact. A puzzled look crossed Deni's face, and she looked at Twain for a second and then took another slice of pizza.

"It's nice having him in the office," Deni said. "But I started there after he'd…checked out, so I didn't have anything to compare it to."

Liv nodded, chewing, trying to keep her hands to herself.

It hadn't been this hard before.

For the first few years, there had been so much anger that wanting to smash Twain's face in was the only physical contact she'd craved. After she'd picked up the pieces of her life, she could acknowledge that she still desired Twain, but not enough to ever put herself in a position to be hurt so badly again.

Was she that twisted that seeing him with another woman was enough to put her back into Twain-yearning mode again so easily? Or was it because it put a crimp in her plans?

The conversation went on, though Liv only paid enough attention to be able to answer when spoken to and laugh at the right time.

And there was plenty of laughter. Twain and Deni—and Matty, for that matter—seemed to have an easy banter and an even easier shared sense of humor.

Had the three of them—Liv, Twain, and Matty—once laughed so loudly and easily together?

Yes. But so many years ago Liv barely remembered it.

"So, you stayed with Beck?" Deni was asking her.

"Pardon?"

"After the divorce? You stayed with the name Beck?"

Liv just numbly nodded and finished off her wine.

"My older brother is going through a divorce right now. Pretty friendly—at least as those things can go. My sister-in-law is trying to decide if she should keep her married name or go back to her maiden name."

"Caleb or Josh?" Twain asked.

"Caleb," Deni answered.

"You didn't tell me that," Twain said to Deni.

She shrugged. "I think it's been in the works for a while, but they didn't want me to worry about it. They didn't tell me until recently."

Twain studied her for a while, making Liv wish she hadn't emptied her wine glass. Then he nodded at Deni, as if he agreed with her family's decision not to tell her about her brother's divorce.

Wait. So Twain knew about her family? Knew the brothers?

"I think I'd like another glass of wine," Liv told the waitress, who was removing one of the pizza pans they'd finished.

Looking at Deni, she said, "Do they have kids?" Deni shook her head. "That can sometimes make a difference to people. It did to me. I wanted to have the same last name as my son."

"That makes sense," Deni said.

"Besides, do you know how many times I've had to spell Koskela or have it mangled in pronunciation? Beck is nice and simple."

"See," Twain said, gesturing to Deni. "I told you it's a great name—goes with anything. Deni Beck has a great ring."

The new glass of wine arrived, and Liv had to physically refrain from downing the whole glass in one gulp.

"Shut up," Deni said to Twain, throwing a napkin at him, which only made him laugh.

"So, you two are—" Liv started.

"Second glass of wine? Does that mean I get to drive home?" Matty interrupted her, hope in his voice. He had his permit and was trying to get his driving hours in as quickly as possible, though Liv hated for him to be learning during the winter months.

"Yes, you get to drive us home," she said, grateful that he'd stopped her from asking something that perhaps she wasn't ready to know just now.

It had been a lot to take in. Finding out there even *was* a woman in Twain's life. One serious enough to bring around Matty and introduce to Liv. And then to have to watch their obvious connection all evening.

Except…Liv wouldn't bet it was love in Twain's eyes when he looked at Deni. No, it was more like…playful affection.

But then, she'd never really seen Twain in love. How would she know what it looked like?

They soon had all three pizzas devoured, though Liv barely remembered eating. Plans were made for the next Matty exchange, and Liv found herself being driven home by her son. Careful to not be overbearing and make him nervous and yet be aware enough to help him if needed, Liv tried to relax on the short drive from the Commodore to their home in west Houghton.

"Sixth Street was really icy when I went home for lunch," she said. "You might want to go around."

Matty nodded and bypassed the shortest—and steepest—route to their home to enter from a different street and angle.

"So…Deni. She seems nice," she said, trying to sound casual.

"Yeah. She's pretty cool."

"Have you known her a while?" Yes, make it about Matty's relationship with Deni, not Twain's.

"About a month, I guess?"

So, it couldn't be *that* serious, if Matty had only met her a month ago. Or, if Twain had stuck to part of the four-month rule, then he could have been with Deni for over five months.

God, she absolutely hated that she was obsessing over this.

Had that all been because he'd never shown any serious interest in one woman?

Until now.

"...and that's when I met her," Matty was saying, and she realized she'd missed the first part. "And she was pretty down. But I'm not sure if that's because they were broken up or what."

They'd broken up?

"That wasn't long, though. And now they're back together. Pretty tight, too. You should see them together."

She just had, and it had been horrible on several levels. Wait. What? "Sorry, zoned out. See who?"

"Deni and Uncle Sawyer."

"Yeah?" she said noncommittally while the cogs slid into place in her mind.

"I mean, I remember Aunt Molly, but I was pretty little when she died."

"Five. You were five," she said, vividly remembering that horrible time in the Beck family, when Molly had died and Sawyer had pulled away from everyone.

"Right. So, I remember her, but not really well. I mean, like, I'm sure she was nice and all, but I really like Deni."

The last cog clicked for Liv. "Deni and your Uncle Sawyer." She tried not to put any questioning in her voice, pretty well convinced that she'd finally caught on.

"It's great to see Uncle Sawyer so happy. I mean, he's always nice to me, but just...you know."

"Yes, I know." Sawyer had always been good to Liv too, even after the divorce. But they didn't see him very often.

Her happiness for Sawyer was hastily pushed aside by her relief that it was he, and not Twain, who was seeing Deni.

Matty did a good job easing into their garage, and Liv praised her son's driving.

Then, after he went into the house, she sat alone in the car until well after the heat dissipated.

Learning that Deni was Sawyer's girlfriend and not Twain's should have elated her. And in some ways, it did. Not in the jealous ways, but because now there was hope that her plan could actually move forward.

Now, if she could just get up the courage to ask Twain for the biggest favor of his life.

Three

"SHE'S REALLY PRETTY," DENI SAID TO TWAIN AS THEY watched Liv and Matty walk out of the Commodore.

"Yeah," Twain answered, relieved when Deni's phone went off and he didn't have to elaborate further.

"Hey," she said softly, and Twain knew it was his brother on the line. "We're still here. Just finishing up. Why don't I order you a meatloaf sub? Have you eaten?" She listened for a moment, nodding to a man who couldn't see her. "Okay. See you soon." She disconnected, a dopey smile on her face. The same smile Sawyer was permanently wearing these days. "He's in Chassell, just finished up. I'm going to order him dinner. But you don't have to stay."

"It's okay, I don't have to be anywhere," he said, and motioned for the waitress to come back over.

Deni ordered a sandwich for Sawyer and another beer for herself, so Twain got one too.

"Really, he'll be here any minute. And even if not, I'm okay to be in a restaurant by myself, you know." She sounded a tiny bit defensive.

He leaned forward, put a hand on her shoulder, and squeezed. Then he sat back in his chair, stretching out his long legs now that Matt wasn't across from him any longer. "You're doing me a favor," he said.

"How?" She sounded skeptical.

"I hate going back home after I've dropped Matt off." It was true, but he was shocked he'd said it out loud. He barely admitted it to himself.

But he and Deni had formed a fast and strong bond, and he wasn't surprised when she gave him a sympathetic nod and stayed silent.

"She reminds me of someone famous," Deni said, changing the subject. Well, changing it back to Liv, which wasn't really any better in Twain's mind. "That woman from *Love Actually*."

"Claudia Schiffer," Twain said.

"I don't know her name."

"It's Claudia Schiffer. She was a supermodel way before *Love Actually* came out."

"Oh, right. That's whom Liam Neeson is talking about when he describes the only woman he'd be interested in. I guess I never put it together that it was the same woman."

He looked at Deni with incredulity and then remembered she was younger than he was by about eight years—making her twelve years younger than Sawyer. Not that it seemed to matter much to them. It didn't to Twain either, not after seeing how happy Deni Casparich made his big brother.

She was also a big engineering geek, so he wasn't too surprised that she'd missed out on some of the pop culture from her childhood.

"Anyway. Liv looks like her."

"Yeah, kind of," he said. Of course she did, though Liv was a tiny thing with no supermodel height. But the same hair, the same startling blue eyes, even the same shy smile. It had been adorable on a cute Liv when they'd first started dating, but she'd grown into a very pretty woman over the years. A fact Twain both admitted to himself and tried to ignore.

What good would it do him?

"Do you guys have a lot of contact? I know you're both really hands-on with Matt, but…"

"Not a lot. Mostly at Matt's meets and stuff. Probably less

once Matt has his license and the drop-offs and pick-ups lessen. We mostly talk on the phone and text about Matt's schedule."

"Well, you seem pretty civil. But maybe that's what happens after…how many years?"

"Seven."

"Right. God, I hope it doesn't take Caleb and Marie seven years to get to a good place."

"It took us about two. Two years to get past all the stuff… that went down."

He could tell she wanted to ask more. And he would have told her whatever she wanted to know, that was how much he liked his brother's girlfriend. And that was saying a lot, because Twain didn't talk about his divorce with anyone. Not even his brothers.

"This is *so* not my business, but…" She waited, and Twain motioned for her to continue, bracing himself with a swig of beer. "I think she still…has feelings for you."

He almost choked on the beer bottle. Careful not to spit out his beer, he slowly swallowed and set the bottle down as Deni picked hers up and studied him while she drank.

"Nope, you read that wrong. There's emotion there, but it ain't love. She hates me."

"I don't think so."

"Trust me. She hates me. She's learned to live with it and hide it for Matt's sake—and I appreciate her for that. But it is not positive feelings you picked up on."

She tilted her head to the side, measuring his words as she continued to stare at him.

"I don't know. When you told her about Sawyer going back to the office, she put her hand on your arm. It seemed like a really natural movement for her."

Demonstrating, Deni leaned forward and placed a hand on his arm. It was a nice, friendly type of touch, and caused nothing like the strange sensations he'd felt when Liv had done the exact same thing earlier.

"She's really fond of Sawyer," he said to Deni. "Just happy to know he was back at work."

She kept her hand on his arm, giving him a little tweak. "It was more than that, it was—"

"Christ, if he's not carrying you to the shower, you're feeling him up in the middle of the Commodore. Can't you two ever keep your hands off each other?" his brother Sawyer said from behind him, as he good-naturedly swatted the back of Twain's head.

"Hey, you. That was fast," Deni said, taking her hand from Twain's arm and reaching out for Sawyer, who leaned down to kiss her before shrugging out of his coat and sitting down across from Twain.

"The thought of a meatloaf sub had me lead-footing it," Sawyer said to Deni, and then leaned over and brushed a longer kiss on Deni's mouth. Twain looked away but heard Sawyer whisper, "Or maybe it was the thought of seeing you."

A knot formed in Twain's throat. He was happy for his brother, rejoiced that Sawyer was back amongst the living after ten years of self-enforced solitude. And Sawyer couldn't have found anybody better than Deni to come out of the cave for.

So why did Twain suddenly feel so shitty?

TWAIN MOTIONED TO MATT on the snowmobile behind his to slow down and pull over. He saw Matt wave back, so he edged off the side of the path he'd created on Toivo Juntunen's property a few days ago and cut his engine, his son doing the same alongside him.

It was Saturday, and though Twain didn't expect it from his crew, he liked working on the weekends because then Matty could join him.

He knew he'd eventually lose his son to friends and—dear God—a girlfriend on the weekends. But for now, Matty still liked joining Twain at his work. Especially when it involved snowmobiling in the woods.

Matt. He had to remember to think of his son as Matt now.

The kid, who was now drinking hot chocolate out of the thermos he'd pulled from his snowmobile's storage, was growing up fast. His requested name change came about the same time he got his learner's permit, though Twain didn't think the two were connected. Just one more broken link in the chain of childhood.

"Did you see the burls on that tiger maple tree?" Matt asked him, dragging the sleeve of his jacket across his mouth, erasing the slight chocolate mustache that Twain had found endearing since his son had been three.

"I did," he answered, and then dug out his own thermos and took a drink of his coffee.

"Can you keep that one?"

Twain nodded. "It's in the bid that I'm writing up for Toivo. I don't think he'll have a problem with it."

"You've already written the bid?"

Twain shook his head. "It's not totally done. That's why I wanted to ride the property one last time. Get some better measurements and counts."

Matt nodded, drank again, and then dug out from the storage area the lunch that Twain had packed him. Ham sandwiches, a bag of chips, and some Oreos Twain had thrown in a baggie.

Matt started in on a sandwich like he had on the pizza the other night at the Commodore.

Which brought back thoughts of Liv. Or, more accurately, thoughts of what Deni had said about Liv having feelings for him.

The crushing guilt for what happened seven years ago rushed through him, but this time he easily swept it away.

Guilt. Anger. Shame. None of it was helpful then, and it hadn't done him much good in the passing years.

He thought he'd let it go. Months would go by without those emotions popping up when seeing or talking with Liv. But then he'd run into someone who would slyly mention the fact that he was divorced...and all that entailed.

Hell, even last week in the Cat's Meow Petey had said in a

roundabout way that if he'd married as young as Twain had, he probably would have cheated on his wife, too.

The coffee suddenly tasted bitter and had cooled off considerably from opening the thermos, so Twain poured it out onto the snow, watching the dark liquid stain the pristine white, almost like blood.

Was Deni right? Did Liv having feelings for Twain other than disdain and dimmed-over-time hatred? There had been his feeling the other night that she'd wanted to talk to him about something.

Did it even matter?

"What will you make with it?" Matt said, pulling him out of his thoughts. Good thing, too, because he didn't really want to answer that last question, even if only to himself.

"Huh? Make out of what?"

"The tiger maple burl. If Toivo lets you have it."

Burls were growths on trees that started as some kind of deformation, like a tumor. Sometimes they were caused by fungus or injury. Though rare, Twain had come across several over the years. Most often, he found them on the roots beneath the ground when he had dug up whole root systems.

Ugly as sin from the outside, but once crosscut, the "deformity" created intricate and beautiful designs that made stunning pieces. It was one of the many things Twain loved about nature—her ability to fool you with ugliness on the outside but devastate you with the beauty underneath.

Most burls were of the size for nice bowls or platters, but the one on the tiger maple Twain had seen on Toivo's property could create something more sizable. He'd been honest in his bid for Toivo and let him know that woodworkers in other areas would pay up to two hundred dollars a pound for the burl. Twain had knocked off the value of the burl from his bid. If he got the job, he'd have the burl to use as he wanted.

"I was thinking of it for the center of a bar."

"For your house?"

"No."

"For Mom's house?"

He looked at his son, confused. "No. For the public. For a driving range Petey Ryan is building. They want to put a bar in it, and he asked me to build it."

"Oh," Matt said, and returned to his sandwich.

"Why did you ask if it was for your mom's house? Does she *need* something made?"

Twain hadn't spent a lot of time in Liv's house over the years, and most of it had been in the kitchen as he waited for Matt. But he'd been in on the designing phase of it. It was a lovely home in west Houghton that was being built when all hell broke loose. They'd lived in an apartment their first eight years of marriage, saving money for a house and putting as much as they could into the logging business so Twain could become partners with Eddie and eventually buy him out.

Liv had moved into it with Matt when it was ready. By then, they'd been separated and barely speaking, so Sawyer did any of the work that needed to be done after the builders were done.

"No, we don't need anything built. It's just…"

"What?" he asked Matt.

His kid shrugged and studied his sandwich—his third—and then answered Twain without looking up. "I don't know. Mom really likes the stuff you made her from tiger maple. She saves the salad bowl set that you made from a tiger maple burl for special occasions."

"She should; that's a pretty rare wood. You wouldn't want to throw those things in a dishwasher every night."

"She doesn't ever put them in the dishwasher. Those have to be washed by hand." He said it with the defeated attitude of the one who always had to do the washing.

"That's good."

"It's just that she really loves them. And the jewelry box and the table. Anything you made out of the tiger maple."

"It's a pretty wood," Twain said softly. When he looked up, Matt was staring at him with an almost accusatory look.

"That's not why she loves them."

No. It wasn't. Twain remembered the joy on Liv's face when he'd brought home the maple pieces he'd made for her over the years they'd been married. He'd almost felt guilty when she'd gush about how pretty they were, how perfect.

She loved him so much, and he made her things from wood. That probably summed up their entire marriage.

"The other night? When we were all at the Commodore?" Matt said.

"Yeah?"

"She sat in the car for a long time after we got home. Just sat there in the garage."

"Was she sick or something?" She'd had two glasses of wine and very little pizza.

"No. I think...I think she thought Deni was *your* girlfriend."

"What? How?" Matty just shrugged while Twain played the night over in his head. Deni had introduced herself, and they had joked about her taking the name Beck. Had Sawyer even come up? Yes, Twain was sure of it. Deni had used that she worked for Sawyer as a way to deflect when Liv asked where they'd met.

And good thing too, because Liv didn't need to know that the first time Twain saw Deni he was breaking into her house, at Sawyer's request, to make sure she was all right during a bad bout with seasonal affective disorder.

But no, Matt was right. It never really came up that Sawyer was the man Deni loved.

"Did you tell her about Deni and Uncle Sawyer?" he asked Matt.

He nodded. "Yes. That's when I realized she must have thought it was you."

"Why?" He didn't want to ask, didn't want to drag his son into anything between Liv and himself. They'd been very careful not to do that. But he desperately wanted to know what had brought Matt to this conclusion.

"I don't know. She seemed...kind of...relieved, I guess."

Matt studied him for a second and then, with the attention span of a fifteen-year-old boy, shrugged, put his garbage back into the storage compartment, and readied himself to ride again.

Twain watched his son leave on the snowmobile, then reached for his own helmet and set off to join Matt.

And to stop thinking about Liv.

Four

—w—

LIV WATCHED FROM THE WARMTH OF THE CHALET AS Matty finished his practice run. She'd been to enough of these meets to know exactly when she should venture outdoors to view her son's turn down the hill in real competition.

Not able to see Liv watching him through the tinted windows, Matty waited at the bottom of the hill near the chairlift but made no move to get in line to ride back to the top of the hill.

Liv looked back up the hill to see another skier, this one a girl, judging by the blond ponytail swishing with the wind. She was a good skier, easily making her way through the gates, though with not as much speed and…recklessness as Matty had. She was wearing the race apron of the Copper Country squad, like Matty had on. But her ski boots and poles were a bright purple.

Heather Summers.

The ponytail wasn't the giveaway—too many of the Finnish girls had them—but the purple poles clinched it.

Liv moved to the edge of the seat, her hands stopping the knitting she'd been doing, her attention all on Matty's body language as he watched Heather navigate the hill.

He was leaning forward, resting his weight on his poles, like skiers often did, stretching out his legs as he leaned. Occasionally, he'd slide his skis forward and back, trying to stay louse and warm for his upcoming run.

His head never moved away from Heather as she made her

way down the course and came to a stop beside him.

She leaned over too, matching Matty's pose, and Liv's breath caught as she watched them. Reaching back in her memory, Liv vaguely remembered that Heather Summers was going out with Stevie Robbins, a boy a year ahead of Heather and Matty.

Though "going out with" was more Liv's verbiage than her son's. "Hanging out" was what Matty called it. To Liv's knowledge, Matty hadn't been "hanging out" with anyone yet, but if the way he leaned toward Heather was any indication, that may have changed.

He was fifteen, a sophomore in high school. This was bound to happen. It was a testament to how much Matty loved to ski and work with his father in the woods that it hadn't happened yet. Or maybe it had.

She'd had "the talk" with him and knew Twain had too, but Liv made a mental note to ask Twain if Matty had told him anything about a girl.

A pang went through her, but she was hard-pressed to identify the emotion.

She just added it to the pile of emotions she'd been feeling for the past three months, since she and Kevin had broken up and she'd come to the realization that she needed to change her—

"Hey, Liv, I didn't miss Matt's run, did I?" Sawyer Beck interrupted her thoughts—thankfully!—and eased his long body onto the hard plastic seat next to her.

"No. He's over there," Liv said, pointing to Matty, who was now just getting on the chairlift. With Heather. "He just finished his last practice run."

"Great," Sawyer said. Glancing at her near-empty cup, he stood back up and said, "I'm going to get a coffee. Want another?"

She nodded, her eyes not leaving her son and his…teammate as they slowly rode up the hill. "Thanks," she said, but Sawyer had already left to go to the concession counter.

Matty and Heather had risen out of Liv's sight and were now safely off the chairlift. Normally, a tiny sigh of relief would sweep over Liv, like it did every time her son rode the sweeping heights of the lift, but this time no relief came.

"I think Matty likes a girl," she said absently to Sawyer when he sat back down, handing her a fresh coffee. He'd obviously remembered how she took hers—the beverage was so light it might have been chocolate milk. She knew when she tasted it she would find he'd also remembered the two packets of sugar she required for her coffee. Well, for her heavily sweetened milk with a dash of coffee. "Thanks," she said, and then took a sip. Yep, good old Sawyer. Ten years basically comatose, but he still knew how she needed her fix.

He waved away her thanks and said, "Back to Matt. Who's the girl?"

She motioned to the hill, which at this time encompassed about fifty high school kids, numerous parents, and coaches. "One of the girls on the Copper Country team."

From the corner of her eye, she saw Sawyer nod and sip from his coffee. Remembering the connection and what Deni had said last week about Sawyer being back at work, she said, "It's Heather Summers."

"Really? God, she would be that old, wouldn't she? Yeah, I remember Andy mentioning that recently. I haven't seen her in a long time, but she always seemed like a good kid."

Liv didn't say anything to that, which was enough for Sawyer to chuckle and throw an arm around her, pulling her close to him for an affectionate squeeze. "I get it, Liv. No girl will be good enough for Matty, right."

Right. "Oh, God, I won't be one of those mothers, will I? The kind who think that her baby shouldn't date because no girl is good enough for him. I couldn't do that to him. Could I?"

She looked at Sawyer, taking comfort in his bemused grin. "No. No way will you be that mother. It's just a shock when it eventually comes, that's all. You'll be fine with it, once you've gotten used to it. It had to happen eventually, right?"

She nodded. Sawyer gave her a good-natured kiss on the top

of her head, took his arm from around her, and put both hands around his paper cup of coffee.

Sawyer had always been good to Liv, periodically helping out around the house after she and Twain had divorced. And even reclusive as he was, he had made an effort to be at most of Matty's pivotal moments. And even some not-so-pivotal, like freezing at a ski meet.

When Molly, Sawyer's wife, had been alive, she and Sawyer had helped a younger Twain and Liv when they could with dinners out for both couples and taking Matty overnight from time to time so Liv and Twain could...reconnect. The two couples couldn't have been more different, and Liv always felt inferior to the polished, educated Molly Beck, though Molly had always been warm and welcoming to her.

She used to feel that Sawyer and Molly might have resented Liv for Twain having to give up Tech and hockey, though they never showed it.

Projection, her therapist had called it. Not Sawyer and Molly's feelings at all, but Liv's.

She took a deep breath and exhaled, a sense of calm coming over her as she realized how far she'd come in the past seven years. She no longer had those types of thoughts, thank goodness. She had shed most of her insecurities and was a much stronger woman now, a woman she was proud of. A woman who knew what she wanted.

Now, she just had to be brave enough to get it.

"So, I heard you met Deni?" Sawyer said.

Taking a sip of coffee, she nodded. After swallowing, she said, "I did. She seems really nice, Sawyer."

He was staring out the huge windows, looking toward the hill, but Liv thought that he wasn't really seeing anything before him. His sight was full of Deni. A huge smile crossed his face as he turned his head to Liv. "She is. Really nice, that is." Then he got what Liv could only call a twinkle in his eyes. "Well, she's not always nice. Sometimes she's very stubborn and downright obstinate." He said it with pride and admiration, like some other man might talk about his girlfriend's smoking hot body.

In just the little bit of time Liv had spent with Deni, she could tell the woman was worlds apart from Molly. But that seemed to be working for Sawyer.

She nudged his shoulder with her own. "That's great, Sawyer. It's so good to see you this happy." It was the truth. She'd seen Sawyer smile over the past ten years, usually when he was with Matt or winning an argument over Twain. But never since Molly had died had Liv seen this spark in Sawyer's eyes.

The man was in love, plain and simple.

And although it was unfair to compare, and she felt a little disloyal to Molly even doing it, she wasn't sure she'd seen Sawyer this happy with even Molly.

And Liv had been around them when they'd been happy—before Molly's depression had taken its toll. And then taken her life.

"Yeah, it feels great. Kind of scary, though, you know?"

Years of living with her Pet Rock of fear of losing Twain had Liv nodding in agreement. "Yes. It can be really scary."

"But worth it."

Liv looked at the top of the hill, unable to make out Matt at this distance but knowing he was up there. Her son. "Yes. Definitely worth it."

"She'll keep me on my toes, that's for sure," Sawyer said.

Looking away from the hill and to her ex-brother-in-law, she said, "Really? I can't imagine a woman ever really keeping you in line."

Or Twain, for that matter. Or Huck, once she thought about it. The Beck brothers were independent men who liked their own company and who seemed most at ease when they were alone. Usually out in the woods somewhere.

That was another thing Liv had come to terms with during her growth. Twain hadn't been trying to get away from her. He just enjoyed being alone in the forests. It had nothing to do with her, though it had stung mightily while they'd been married.

"Oh yeah, she's got my number, that's for sure," he said, chuckling a little, causing Liv to turn to look more closely at the handsome man.

Handsome, yes, but never as attractive to her as Twain, though they did share quite a few physical similarities.

Not looking at her, but sensing Liv's attention, Sawyer went on. "When we first got together, I kind of blew it. Freaked out over something that, looking back, was something we can easily handle...together."

Liv waited for him to go on. Natural curiosity wanted her to ask what the issue had been, but she didn't want to make Sawyer uncomfortable. Not when he was opening up to her more than he had in the past ten years. "Anyway, when I tried to make it better, or at least get past it, she let me have it." He took a sip of his coffee, then kept his hands still on the cup as he held it between his opened legs, his elbows resting on his knees. "She told me—in no uncertain terms—exactly what she needed from me, what she felt it would take to be in a relationship with her. And if I wasn't up for the job, she'd move on."

"Wow," Liv said, impressed with Deni's guts. "How old is she?"

Sawyer barked a laugh. "I know. She's twenty-eight. The age difference doesn't bother her, so I'm certainly not going to dwell on it."

"No, it's not that," Liv said. "Who cares about that kind of stuff?"

"You'd be surprised."

"No. I meant to have that kind of insight at that age. To be able to tell you that's how she felt. And really, to risk losing you. I don't think I could have been that honest, with myself or... anyone else, at that age. I'm barely able to now." But she knew she could. She'd have to in order to get what she wanted.

"It's not like you're ancient, Liv. You're what, thirty-five? Six?"

"Thirty-five. But still. Even seven years ago... *Especially* seven years ago, I wouldn't have been able to do that. I think it's great that she could."

"She's special, that's for sure. But she also has a pretty analytical mind. She just explained the facts to me and let me decide. And at first, I disappointed her."

"Oh," Liv said, surprised. Sawyer had always been very sure of himself. Always been in control. Even during his reclusiveness after Molly's death, Liv got the feeling that Sawyer knew exactly what he was doing. To know that he'd stumbled with Deni early on was somehow…reassuring to Liv.

"But then I came around," Sawyer said, smiling. He took another drink from his cup, draining it. "In fact, Twain was instrumental in helping me see the light."

"Really?"

He nodded. "Yep. He knocked some sense into me. Literally." He stood, cup in hand. "I'm getting a refill. Need one?"

She shook her head. Her second cup was still more than half-full, and she'd be out on the hill, away from a restroom.

As Sawyer left, she thought again about how brave Deni had been to spell out to the man she loved what exactly it would take to keep her.

Liv had never been that brave. Early on, it was because she hadn't been capable of it—her Pet Rock outweighing any gumption she might have had. Then, when she'd been able to throw the rock from her back, there'd never really been anyone she wanted so badly that she'd fight to keep.

Even Kevin Schmidt, whom she'd been with for two years and almost married.

If she'd been able to articulate her needs the way Deni had when Liv had been married to Twain, would things be different now? If she'd been able to even *know* what she needed, would that awful, awful day ever had happened?

Would Matty have both his parents under one roof and not be shuttled back and forth between them? Would they have a houseful of children?

Who knew? And it was fruitless to beat herself up about it now—or to even remember the day that her life fell apart.

Could she tell Twain exactly what she needed from him? Would she be able to do that now—when she had so much riding on it?

And what would he say when she told him?

Five

—◦◦◦—

WHEN TWAIN WALKED INTO THE CHALET AT THE SKI
hill, his eyes found his brother walking away from the concession
stand. Sawyer caught Twain's eye, nodded toward where Liv sat,
and then turned around and went back to the concession counter,
presumably to get a cup of coffee for Twain. Bless him.

Making his way through the large—blessedly heated—room,
Twain nodded and murmured hellos to other parents, not really
interacting with them.

He was younger than most of them, and he and Liv had never
been the types to hang with the group, even when they'd been
married. By the time Matt was old enough to ski competitively,
Twain and Liv had buried the past, got along well, and had been
sitting together at all of Matt's events. He knew that it was a topic
of gossip amongst the other parents, but he didn't give a shit.

It gave them a chance to talk about Matt, Matt's schedule, or
whatever was going on with their son. Plus, he'd always enjoyed
Liv's company. Once she'd been able to stomach the sight of him
again, they'd fallen into a nice friendship. Or at least friendly co-
parenting.

Sawyer often joined them at things like this, and tiny Liv,
just an inch or two over five feet, always sat between them, as if
being bookended by giants.

"Hey," he said as he rounded the seat next to Liv. The one
without Sawyer's scarf along the back. A scarf Liv had knitted.

"Hi," she said, looking up at him, a smile on her face. On her adorable face.

No, not adorable anymore, he thought as he took his seat, shedding the layer of the warm coat he wore while working. Liv had been impossibly cute in high school, her blindingly blue eyes following his every move, even before the night at Paula Ilonen's party when they first hooked up. But now, Liv's cherubic cuteness had grown into striking beauty, high cheekbones replacing plump cheeks. Her eyes were still blindingly blue, but were now full of knowledge, and maybe just a touch of weariness, instead of being open and inquisitive.

And they certainly didn't follow his movements any longer.

Or did they? He hadn't forgotten what Matt had said the other day about Liv thinking Deni was Twain's girlfriend. In fact, that conversation, and the unanswered questions Twain had about it, had come to him with horrifying frequency.

"I take it that I made it in time," he said as Sawyer returned, handed him a cup of coffee, and took the seat on the other side of Liv.

"Yes," Liv said. The buzz of her phone sounded from her pocket. She set down her cup on the little table in front of them, next to her knitting, and pulled the phone out. "Matty. He's racing twentieth."

Both Twain and his brother nodded, taking drinks from their cups. They had time before they needed to put on their coats, go outside, and climb up the hill a hundred yards or so to get a better vantage point to watch Matt's first run.

"And how high does he have to place to qualify for U.P. finals?"

"Fifth," Liv and Twain both said in answer to Sawyer's question.

"What kind of shot does he have?" Sawyer asked.

Liv looked at Twain before she spoke. "He's got a chance, but he'll really have to ski his best. There are some senior boys that will be tough to beat." She looked at Twain again, as if for reassurance.

He nodded at her. "He's got this."

A smile came over her face, and Twain felt his insides go a little soft. And a little hard a bit farther south.

Before he could think on it further, she turned from him and picked up her knitting, something she did almost all the time when her hands weren't busy with something else. Like work, or cooking, or driving.

Or him. Her hands had always been plenty busy with him.

Years ago. Many years ago. Christ, where were these thoughts coming from?

He tried to watch the skiers, now coming down the hill one at a time. Gracefully—and sometimes not so gracefully—making their way through the tight slalom course.

And yet his eyes continued to slide down and away from the window to Liv's hands as she continued to knit. Tiny hands, moving as smoothly as the skiers glided on the snow.

Those small hands sliding all over his big body.

"Pete Ryan may be contacting you," Sawyer said, looking over Liv's head to Twain, pulling him out of thoughts about what types of things Liv used to do with those clever, clever hands.

"About the bar? Yeah, I saw him last week, and he mentioned it."

Sawyer looked back to the hill, nodding. "Good. It's a tight project, so not a lot of room for frills, but he'll pay you a fair price."

Liv's hands stilled for a second, her thumb rubbing back and forth on her needle.

"Pete Ryan and some guy are building an indoor driving range," Twain explained to her, though she hadn't asked. "Summers and Beck are building it. If he gets a liquor license for it, he wants a bar made. Kind of a specialty piece."

She nodded, her fingers moving once more upon the yarn, needles making a soft clacking that Twain should have found annoying, but which had always calmed him. "You'll make a beautiful one for him," she said.

"I said yes, but it's not a done deal. It would be a fun project, though. A little break, something I could do when I'm not in the woods. Maybe Matt could help me with it."

A soft smile played along the corner of her mouth on the side Twain could see. "He'd like that."

"There are a few tiger maples on some property I have a bid on. They'd be perfect for it," he said to Sawyer. "One has a burl on it about four feet long. I'm going to amend the bid to do those trees on a side basis." Sawyer was nodding, but Liv's hands had stilled once more, the needles lowering to her lap as she looked up and to the hill. Twain didn't think she was watching the skiers.

Was it the wood? Had mentioning it brought up memories of the things he'd made for her, like it had for Matt last week? She moved her head forward just enough that her long blond hair fell like a curtain in front of her face, preventing Twain from being able to read any possible expression.

"Umm...there would probably be enough lumber for the bar and some left over," he said, not really knowing why. "If you need, or want, anything for your house..."

She quickly looked up at him, the hair returning to its natural place, allowing him to see her face. "Thank you. That's very...nice of you. I can't think of anything that I need."

Twain shrugged. "Keep it in mind. We've got time before I get to it, if I even do."

She nodded and continued to look at him. He waited, meeting her gaze, their years together—and apart—telling him she had more to say. Something she was having trouble with. When they were first together, he would try to coax things out of her. Later, he'd be exasperated by her reticence. But now, he just waited patiently for her to go on.

She opened her mouth and then must have thought better of it. With the tiniest of head shakes—seemingly more to herself than to him—she looked away from him and raised her knitting once again.

"How many is that?" Twain asked, motioning to the most

recent racer to pass the finish line. He tried to hide from his voice any hurt he felt from Liv's inability to talk to him.

Things were so different between them now, and yet some things were so familiar. His attraction to her. Her never feeling comfortable enough to truly speak her mind to him, for fear that she'd hurt him or anger him—or, shit, rock the boat in any way.

It was what it was.

The boat had been rocked. Hell, it had capsized on them. And yet they were still here, together, civil, watching their greatest achievement—Matt.

"That was twelve," the ever-correct Sawyer said, rising from his seat. "Probably time to get out there."

The three of them made their way to a good vantage point on the hill and waited, stamping feet and rubbing gloved hands together for warmth.

A flash burst through Twain's brain of how Liv used to warm his hands up when he'd come home from a long day in the woods, nearly causing him to lose his footing.

"Careful," Liv said, grabbing his arm. As if her small body would stop him from falling down the hill if he was going down. Still, it felt good, even through all the layers, and he took his time regaining his balance.

"This should be Matt," Sawyer said. Twain didn't have to bother with something as simple as counting kids down a hill when his engineer-geek brother was around.

Sure enough, his son moved into position at the starting gate, and Twain held his breath as Matt skied his way down the hill. When he passed the three of them, Liv put a hand on both his and Sawyer's arms and squeezed.

"He's doing great," she exclaimed, voicing the excitement that Twain felt.

Matt, being a typical teenager, basically ignored their presence from the bottom of the hill while he waited for his time and standing to be shown on the portable electronic board. When it came up, Twain couldn't see it from his angle, but Matt's fist pump in the air told him all he needed to know. Matt did give a nod to them before making his way back to the chairlift for his second run.

The idea that his baby boy was this old, and this accomplished, awed Twain, and he found himself taking Liv's hand beside him.

She looked up at him and smiled, seeming to know what he was feeling. A sheen of moisture glistened in her eyes.

"We did good," he said softly to her as another kid on skis whizzed by them.

An actual tear dropped down to her reddened-by-the-cold cheek as she nodded in agreement. "We sure did," she said back.

Again, she had that moment of wanting to say more, like when they'd been in the chalet. And like then, she seemed to think better of it—whatever *it* was—and turned her gaze back to the hill.

"Looks like we'll be going to Marquette," she said.

Though it would be a hassle taking time away from logging, there was no way Twain would miss seeing his kid ski at the U.P. finals.

Spending more time with Liv wouldn't be too awful, either.

Six

LIV RAISED HER GLASS OF WINE, BUT BEFORE SHE COULD take that first, much-needed sip, Sawyer raised his beer bottle in toast and declared, "To Matt. May he ski as well tomorrow as he did today."

Twain and Deni also raised their bottles, and the four of them clinked in honor of her son's good day of preliminary skiing.

He had done well enough to qualify to ski in two events tomorrow, Sunday, at the finals. He'd been disappointed, hoping to final in three events, but Liv couldn't have been more proud of her son.

Neither could Twain, if his grin and slightly teary eyes were any indication.

"To Matt," he said, looking at her as he drank from his beer.

They all put their beer bottles down and started looking at the menu. Liv hung on to her wine glass for a couple more sips.

They were at a restaurant in Marquette that a coworker had suggested when Liv mentioned they'd be there for the weekend.

It was nice that Sawyer and Deni had come to watch Matty compete, even staying for both days. Matty appreciated it, Liv knew, but so did she. It felt natural to be having dinner with the three of them, even though she'd only met Deni Casparich once before.

But seeing how happy she made Sawyer—and it was obvious how head over heels he was—put Deni at the top of Liv's list.

Matty was having dinner with the family of his closest friend on the team, Justin, who had also qualified to ski at the U.P. finals.

Liv was quietly pleased that Heather Summers hadn't qualified and wouldn't be in Marquette competing. Plenty of time to deal with that kind of monitoring once she'd had a chance to talk with Matty about Heather.

She'd tried a couple of times over the past week, but Matty had quickly shut her down each time.

After dinner, the boys would then bunk with Twain in his room for the night. Liv and Twain would have dinner on their own, and the other parents got their room to themselves that night. Nobody would even consider Liv and Twain sharing a room, so it seemed like a win-win for everyone.

"He's such a good kid. Matt," Deni said, while perusing her menu. She looked up at Liv and added, "You've done such a great job. Really. Great kid."

"Thank you," Liv said.

"What the hell am I? Chopped liver?" Twain said with mock indignation.

Deni rolled her eyes at him. Placing her menu down on the table and closing it, she said, "Yes, Daddy, you did good, too. But I was thinking more about how well-mannered he is and his comfort talking with adults. Stuff I'm guessing he got from Liv, based on what I know about the Beck brothers."

"Hey!" both Sawyer and Twain said to her.

"I've got good manners," Sawyer said, placing his elbows on the table to look at Deni.

"And I can complete a full sentence and carry on a conversation with an adult," Twain said.

Deni nodded. "Yes, but neither of you *like* to."

The brothers looked at each other and grinned. Liv took a sip of her wine. Better that than to openly gasp at the sheer magnitude of the handsome brothers at ease, guards down and with those smiles.

"Holy wah," Deni said, looking at her man and his brother.

Then she looked at Liv. "Talk about high voltage, eh?"

Liv didn't pretend to misunderstand the younger woman. "I'll say. You should see them when all three are together. It's the same result as wearing an estrogen patch."

Deni nearly spat out the beer she was sipping, a laugh constricting her ability to swallow. Dabbing at her mouth with a napkin, she said, "Is that right? I have yet to see the complete trio of Beck Brothers together."

"No? It's a sight."

"I haven't even met Huck yet."

"He doesn't look a thing like Sawyer and Twain. Blond. Blue-eyed. But just as…Beck as these two."

"What are they talking about?" Sawyer said to Twain.

"How hot we are," Twain explained, his grin going even wider and a little bit…naughty.

Even though it had been years, that old familiar reaction to that particular grin of Twain's rushed through Liv, making her skin tingle. And other places.

"Oh, that," Sawyer said, waving a hand. Then he reached out and slid his hand down Deni's ponytail, letting it stay on the back of her chair. Deni smiled at him. A smile that said the night was only beginning for them.

Twain watched them and then looked over at Liv. His bright green eyes were sharp and held many emotions.

The look said so much to Liv. That Twain was happy his brother was back amongst the emotionally living and deeply in love. (Liv was happy for Sawyer, too.) That it felt good to him to be enjoying this dinner with this group of people. (It did to Liv, too.) That it had been a good day. (Yep, for Liv, too.)

But mostly, what she read in Twain's eyes was yearning.

Not necessarily for Liv. But for what Sawyer and Deni shared. (Ditto.)

Twain's eyes, a green that changed depending on his emotions, from the color of summer grass to that of the clearest emerald, had always been easy for Liv to read.

Stoic and alpha in most ways, his eyes always gave away his true emotions. At least to her.

It was why when they'd been married, she had started looking away from him when she told him she loved him.

And they weren't saying "it" now, but the way he looked at her, with desire mixed with regret, had her believing he still had some feelings for her.

Which would serve her well, if she could ever get up the nerve to ask him for what she really wanted.

Deni quit drinking after her first beer, declaring herself their designated driver, so the other three indulged in wine with their steak dinners.

On the drive back to the hotel, Liv received a text from Susan Porter, the mother of the friend Matty was having dinner with.

"The Porters just deposited Matty and Justin in your room," she said to Twain as she texted back that they were on their way to the hotel.

"God, that's one way to kill this nice buzz," Twain said. "Two fifteen-year-old boys 'Dude!'ing as they show each other cool stuff on their phones."

They all chuckled, Liv especially. Because Twain had certainly nailed it, and, oh yeah, she had a nice, healthy buzz going too. She found everything anybody was saying quite funny.

"Your giggle was always so damn cute," Twain said quietly. He was sitting in the back seat of Deni's Subaru next to her.

"A woman my age should be beyond giggling," Liv said, though she'd loved his compliment.

"I say nobody should be beyond giggling," Deni said, pulling into the parking lot of the hotel while brushing Sawyer's hand out of her lap as she'd done several times on the short drive from the restaurant.

"Amen," Sawyer chimed in, putting his big hand high up on Deni's thigh again.

This time she didn't brush it away, but instead gave Sawyer

a playful look as she parked the car and turned off the ignition.

"I know that look. Both of their looks. We'd better leave them here, Liv. Who knows if they'll get to the elevator with all their clothes on."

Liv scrambled out of the back seat, said good night to Deni and Sawyer—who vaguely waved and murmured goodbye while their eyes stayed locked on each other—and allowed Twain to take her arm and guide her into the hotel lobby.

They rode up the elevator in silence, Liv not looking at Twain in case his eyes were at work again, letting her infer things that she had no business thinking.

She went to his room with him to check on Matty. The room was down the hall from hers and had two queen beds as opposed to her one king.

Matt and Justin were each sprawled out, one on each bed, phones on their chests, the Red Wings on TV.

"Dude, did you see that check?" Justin said to Matty even though Matty's eyes were on the television too.

"Totally on his damn ass," Matty replied, and then noticed his parents in the doorway. "Sorry," he said to Liv about the small curse.

"I was just told this evening what a good job your father and I had done raising you because you're so well-mannered," Liv said, giving Matty a playful tweak on the foot as she sat on the bed next to him.

He grinned and knocked his foot into her hip—about as much affection as she got from him these days, especially in front of a friend.

"What did you have for dinner?" she asked him.

"Burger," both boys said. Their phones buzzed at the same time, and after quick glances, they looked at each other. "Dude! No way," Justin said to a grinning Matty, their fingers starting to fly on their respective phones.

Taking off his coat, Twain gave her a "Told you so" eye roll. Liv stood and walked to him where he stood in the entryway.

"Do you want to hang out in my room for a while? Until they crash? It probably won't be long, given the day they had."

They'd been up early to get to Marquette, which was a two-hour drive from Houghton, Matty driving with Liv, and Twain riding with Deni and Sawyer.

He looked at the television longingly. "I'd love to, but I want to watch the game…" He left it out there, with almost…hope in his voice.

"You can watch it in my room. I'm going to knit or read anyway."

And hopefully talk. She'd decided during dinner that if she could get Twain alone this weekend, she was definitely going to ask him. Her plans had been on hold for too long.

"Deal," he said, smiling.

She swallowed, nervous that she would now get the chance she'd been waiting for.

"Your dad will be in my room for a bit. Text or call if you guys need anything."

"Will do," Matty said, not taking his eyes from his phone. Justin only lifted a hand in acknowledgement.

In the hallway, she texted Susan Porter to let her know that they'd just seen the boys and Twain would be in her room watching the hockey game. She didn't think Justin's parents would have a problem with Twain not being in the room with the boys, but if it were her, she'd want to know. In the moments it took to walk the length of the hall to her room, she received an *okay, thanks* text back.

She took her coat off, and after helping her and hanging up the coat, Twain sat on the edge of her bed and flicked on the television, settling the channel on the hockey game.

After they'd been married a few years and Petey Ryan—Twain's former teammate at Tech—was playing in the NHL, it had pained Liv to watch Twain when he had hockey on. He tried to hide it from her, but there was always a wistfulness on his face, especially if he was watching whatever team Petey was playing for.

That was no longer the case, she noticed, watching him now. He obviously still enjoyed the game, but it didn't seem to be as all-encompassing to him as it had.

As if to prove her musings true, he took his eyes from the screen and looked over at her. "What?" he said.

She shook her head. "Nothing. Just… Nothing," she said softly.

He stared at her, his eyes not leaving hers, even though from the sounds coming from the television, somebody had just scored.

"Liv, I…" But he didn't finish what he was saying, just continued to look at her. She'd changed out of her many layers after the meet and before dinner, but she was still wearing leggings and a bulky sweater she'd made. A very high-necked sweater.

But Twain was looking at her like she was wearing some flimsy negligee. And the heat that scorched through her had her wishing she were wearing something that light.

She moved to the dresser and picked up her needles and yarn, feeling his gaze upon her back as she did.

Now. It had to be now or she would lose her nerve. Let the glow of the wine and the good vibes she was feeling from Twain be her guide and get it over with. If he said no, it was better to know that now so she didn't waste any more time.

She put her knitting back down and turned quickly, Twain's gaze coming up from her ass to her eyes just as quickly.

A grin crossed his face, rough and manly with a three-day growth. A grin that said "Busted" but also that he didn't care.

"Twain, I need to ask you something."

"Okay," he said, still grinning. Until he noticed her rubbing her hands on her hips, a habit she had when she was nervous. The grin gone, he leaned forward on the edge of the bed, almost touching her. "Liv?" he said.

"It's more of a favor really," she said, swallowing hard. As much wine as she'd drunk, you wouldn't think her mouth could go this dry.

He reached out, his long arms touching her. He rested a hand on each of hers, stilling their nervous movement. "Anything, Liv. You know that."

Yes, he'd done anything and everything she'd asked of him. When they were married and after.

Except for one thing.

But this wasn't about that. It wasn't even really about Twain. This was for her. And she deserved to have it.

She took a step toward him, his hands staying on her hips even as she took hers and placed them on his shoulders.

"Twain," she said, bolstering herself with a deep breath. "I want another baby."

With the look of shock and confusion just beginning on his face, she added the kicker.

"And I want it to be yours."

Seven

AN ICE BUCKET CHALLENGE TO HIS NUTS COULDN'T have cooled Twain off quicker than Liv's words.

"What's that?" he said, as if he hadn't heard her quite clearly. But he'd heard her. Just to make sure, she said the words again.

"I want to have your baby, Twain."

"Yeah, that's what... Um, yeah."

She sat down next to him on the bed, exactly how he'd envisioned this night going when they'd been at dinner, the fantasy solidifying even more when she'd invited him to her room.

The bed shifted as Liv moved a little closer to him on the bed, bringing Twain back to the matter at hand.

He was not going to sleep with Liv tonight. And maybe never again. Though somewhere in the back of his mind, he hadn't really considered the possibility that he'd never again hold Liv's curvy body in his arms.

But there was something even more important to think about other than not getting laid tonight. Though that ranked right up there.

A baby. She wanted a baby. *His* baby.

Could this be about Kevin and Liv breaking up?

He turned toward her, pulling one of his legs up on the bed so he could fully face her. One thing he'd—belatedly—learned during his marriage: even though *you* think you can talk and listen while you keep an eye on the hockey game, your female companion will disagree.

"Liv, honey," he said, placing a hand on hers. "Is this about you and Kevin? Matt told me you two broke up."

A look of puzzlement crossed her face, making her brow furrow in a way Twain had always found endearing. He had often reached out and placed a finger there, trying to ease her or the mood.

His hand itched to do it now, but he kept still until her expression eased and the puzzlement turned to something he wasn't able to read.

"Maybe. I don't know." Years of marriage to Liv, and the subsequent years of divorce, had taught Twain a few things, and so he waited for Liv to work her thoughts out.

She slid her hand out from under his and placed it in her lap, lacing her fingers together. "It's not about Kevin," she said. "Not Kevin himself. It is about us ending our relationship."

After Matt had told him Liv and Kevin had split, Twain had heard around town that Kevin had cheated on Liv. Knowing the pain and embarrassment she'd gone through when their own marriage had exploded, Twain had felt a deep surge of empathy for her.

And more guilt for himself.

"The reason I was with Kevin, well, not the only reason, but the main one, was I wanted to have another baby."

So, this went further back than just an alarm bell going off when she'd turned thirty-five a couple of months ago.

As if reading his mind, she said, "If I'm being truthful, I've wanted another baby since Matty turned six or seven."

"But we were still married then."

She nodded and waited while Twain flipped back through his mind to those last couple of years of their marriage. "You did mention it a couple of times," he admitted.

"Yes, but you didn't seem very...receptive to the idea at the time."

"No. We were finally on our feet. I'd signed the partnership agreement with Eddie. You'd gone full-time at Tech. Matty was in school. We'd bought the property for the house about then, right?"

She nodded. "Yes. All reasons you brought up at the time to not have another baby. And I didn't argue with any of them. I *couldn't* argue with them because they were valid reasons, and I agreed with them."

"In theory," he said. He vaguely heard a roar coming from the television. Instead of turning to see what had happened, or a replay, he reached for the remote and turned the set off.

Yeah, this was going to take all of his attention. Probably more focus than he was capable of, but he needed to try to understand. For Liv.

He owed her.

"More than theory. I knew you were right. I knew we were in a good place. A place lots of people who get married and have a child so young never even get to."

When she didn't go on, he started for her, "And yet…"

She looked away from him, but he could see the clear blue of her eyes turn a tiny bit darker. And misty. "And yet…I wanted another baby."

He almost reached out for her again but decided to keep his hands to himself. She didn't want his comfort now. She needed it years ago when she'd wanted another child and he hadn't been able to understand how important it was to her.

And the part that made him feel even more like shit was the fact that even if he *had* known how important it was to her, he wasn't sure he would have changed anything.

After he quit Tech, one of Twain's favorite forestry professors had introduced him to Eddie Tuisku, a local who owned a small logging company.

Even though Twain had no experience in logging, other than being able to correctly identify every type of tree—and most plants— Eddie had taken a chance and hired him. The job paid about as well as any other job Twain would be able to pull down in the Copper Country with only a year and a half of college. And it allowed him to be outside, which, other than on the ice playing hockey, was the place Twain most wanted to spend his time. Even in winter.

The work was hard and long, but Twain loved it. By the time Matty was six, Twain and Eddie had agreed to a partnership so that Eddie could retire, since the years of the hard life of logging were beginning to affect his health.

Eddie had no children of his own, was a widower, and wanted Twain to take over the business. Which, with Eddie's guidance, Twain had done, making T&B Logging (changing the name from Tuisku to include Beck after Twain bought in) one of the top logging companies in the U.P.

Missing time with his wife and baby had been a necessary side effect to keeping a roof over their heads and food on the table.

But, yeah, if he was honest with himself, he hadn't minded being in the forest—sometimes alone, sometimes with his crew—all that much. It centered him, allowed him to focus. He felt he was better equipped to deal with a baby and wife when he came home from spending the day in the woods.

The timing hadn't been right when she'd brought it up. But shit, the timing hadn't been right with Matt, and look at how much love Twain had for his son. For his only child.

"Anyway," Liv said with a small wave, looking back at him now as if she had also gone to her own place of remembrance. "I thought I'd have a child with Kevin. That's why I'd even gotten—"

She stopped, and Twain realized she was about to reveal more than she wanted. He shouldn't care about her reasons for getting so serious with Kevin. It didn't affect him at all, but he found that he was dying for the information. "Why you and Kevin got together? Stayed together?" he asked, hoping she'd finish his thoughts.

She shook her head. "It doesn't matter. None of that matters, especially since we're not together anymore."

"Yeah, about that—"

"But when we *were* together, he knew that I wanted another child. We were waiting for the right time, but... You know."

He knew. It hadn't been the right time for him all those years ago, and apparently, it hadn't been the right time for Kevin.

Irrational as it was, he found himself silently loathing Kevin for not making Liv happy.

Not that Twain had.

"Yeah, I know," he said. "Liv, I'm sorry I didn't know how important it was to you back then."

"I didn't push it. I didn't...make my voice heard," she said.

She hadn't been a doormat when they'd been married, but she'd definitely deferred to Twain in most things. Sometimes to Twain's relief, but most times to his frustration. They may have started off in less than ideal circumstances, but Twain had always envisioned marriage as a partnership, and he hadn't liked the idea of making all the decisions alone.

Make my voice heard. It sounded straight from a self-help book, which usually gave Twain the hives. In this case, though, it was totally accurate. Liv didn't allow her voice to be heard.

Until the end. He could sure hear her voice as she screamed at him to get out of their apartment and that their marriage was over.

But now... Now it seemed that Liv had grown into the woman Twain had seen glimpses of in the girl he'd taken home from Paula Ilonen's party all those years ago.

She was "speaking her truth" (was that the touchy-feely way of saying it?) to him now.

"Honestly, Twain, I'm not saying this to make you feel bad about the past."

He studied her pretty face. As always, it was easy to see she was telling the truth, her expression unable to hide anything.

"Thank you," he said. "Lord knows, I will always feel bad about the past. The way I hurt you that night, Liv, I—"

"Like I said, this isn't about the past," she interrupted him, and the look on her face let him know that she in no way wanted to revisit that particular night.

Fine with him.

"And this isn't really even about us—you and me. I only brought that up so you'd know how badly—how long—I've wanted another baby."

"Okay. I remember. And I get it. But Liv—"

"Hear me out." She turned again, pulling her legs fully onto the bed, crossing them at the ankles, and resting her elbows on her knees. It was obvious she was ramping up for a sales pitch that she must have been thinking about for a while.

Twain vaguely wondered if Kevin had gotten the same pitch. And if they had also been on a bed when she'd pitched him. Finding he detested the idea, Twain wiped the quickly forming image from his mind and waved for Liv to continue.

"Yes, I had thought I'd have a child with Kevin. But if he and I aren't going to have a future together—and believe me, there is *no* way that's going to happen—then I'd rather have your baby."

"So, you think—"

"Not that I think *we* have a future together. That's not at all what I'm saying. What I'm asking for."

"It's all about my sperm," he said, trying to put a little levity in the situation, before it turned from absurd to downright surreal. Which would probably happen during the spiel Liv was about to lay on him.

"Yes. We know you have good sperm," she said, teasing in her voice.

Before he could respond to that (and really, what was the proper response?), Liv charged on. "I mean, my God, look at Matty. Is he not just the best kid in the world?"

Twain smiled. "He's pretty great, yeah. But Liv, it hasn't all been smooth sailing. The terrible twos, the falls from trees, the terrible tens, the constant whining for a phone, the terrible twelves. And we're just *getting* to all the teen bullshit he's going to pull on us."

"I'm not delusional, Twain. I know parenting is hard work.

I've done it. Am doing it."

The fact that she'd done most of it with Matty, particularly in the early years while Twain was trying to get established with Eddie, kept him silent.

"I'm not confusing the difficulty or ease—ha!—of parenting with the desire to have another child."

"But diapers? Again? Potty training? You want to go through all that again?"

"Yes," she said without hesitation.

He shook his head. "I don't know if I can, Liv. I was barely able to help you then, and now I'm the owner of the company."

"Look, Twain, I'm not asking you to change diapers, or potty train, or teach her how to ride a bike. I'll do all of that."

"Being a single parent is hard, Liv. We both know that. The shuttling from one house to the other, figuring out schedules, and making each place feel like home. It was so tough on Matty at first, remember?"

She stiffened almost imperceptibly, but Twain knew her well. Knew her body as well as he knew his own. At least he used to.

"Of course I remember," she said, a bit defensively. Then she softened and continued, "But this child won't have that. She'll have never had a father in her life, so she won't know the difference. Or, at least, she won't go through her parents divorcing."

"What do you mean she'll have never had a father in her life?"

Liv shrugged and looked at him like she was about to hurt his feelings and didn't want to.

Shit. "Are you saying this really *is* all about my sperm? And only my sperm?"

"That's entirely up to you. I am prepared to raise this child completely on my own. How much you want to be involved is up to you."

"Seriously?"

"Yes."

"So, what? I go to pick up Matty for the weekend and

here's...*her* standing at the door watching her brother leave with her father while she's not invited? Way to fuck a kid up."

"First of all, she never needs to know that you're her biological father." Twain inwardly bristled at that. "No one would need to know," she added, and this time he outwardly bristled. "Up to you," she said, her hands up in a placating gesture, which only further pissed him off.

"Second," she continued, "Matt will have his license in the summer, and you won't have to pick him up as much, if at all."

He hadn't thought about that, not picking up Matt—and therefore not seeing Liv—in the near future. Finding the thought bothered him more than he cared to admit, he pushed it from his mind, acknowledging that he'd have to examine it later.

"Third, by the time she's old enough to realize that you're Matt's father—and all that entails—Matt will be in college and not even at home."

Ah. "Is that what this is all about? An impending empty nest?"

She seemed surprised at the suggestion, and Twain quickly realized that Liv's desire to have another child went beyond Matty growing up and leaving home.

"No. That's not it at all. I couldn't *replace* Matty with another baby, and I wouldn't want to."

"Is it because you always wanted a girl?" At the look of shock on her face, he continued, "You never said anything, and certainly never showed it, but I knew how disappointed you were that we had a boy."

"For about a minute," she said.

Which was true, but Twain had seen her face—had been holding her exhausted body in his arms—when they'd been told she'd given birth to a son. She'd been devastated. Until they had laid a screaming, wiggling Matty in her arms.

But still...

"No, it's not about wanting a girl. There's obviously a fifty percent chance I'll have another boy."

A twinge went through him as she said "I'll" instead of "we'll" about her child.

"Twain," she said, compassion in her voice. She placed a hand on his knee. "I've wanted another child for a long time. I never would have guessed I'd only have one. I always saw myself with two or three kids."

So had Twain, once upon a time. He only nodded for her to go on.

"After we split up, I thought that maybe I'd have more kids with someone else. When that didn't happen right away, I considered adoption or a sperm bank. Then I met Kevin, and it seemed like we were on track for…a future."

"Did he want kids?" He couldn't help himself from asking, even though it was none of his business. Still, Liv was asking him to become a father again—at the very least a sperm donor—so he should be entitled to ask a personal question or two.

"He said he did. But now I think he was just humoring me and hoping I'd, I don't know, drop it, I guess."

"Like you did with me."

Her blue eyes locked on his. "Yes. But I don't do that anymore. I don't let things that are important to me drop just so I don't…upset the apple cart with the man I'm with."

A lump formed in Twain's throat. He'd always been aware that Liv had given up—or at least changed—her future the same as he had when they'd gotten pregnant. But… "You weren't…afraid of me, were you, Liv? Afraid to tell me things, ask me things?"

She didn't answer right away, and Twain began to feel the familiar tingle of failure he often experienced when thinking about Liv. "No, it wasn't that. I wasn't afraid of you or of talking to you. But I was always afraid that I'd lose you," she said, kind of like she was just now putting it into words for the first time. Maybe she was.

"You weren't going to lose me," he said.

A small, sad smile came to her, and she lifted her hands in defeat, letting them fall to her lap. "I *did* lose you, Twain."

"But that's not why—"

"I'm really sorry. I did not want to go down this road with you. You're a wonderful father to Matty, and if you'd like to be involved in this child's life, that would be great. But you don't have to. In fact, I'm guessing we would want to come to some kind of legal agreement about that. And I certainly wouldn't expect you to pay child support like you do for Matty."

"I would support my child," he said firmly.

"I wouldn't expect it."

"Tough."

"If you agree to this, we can have that discussion."

An image popped into his head. One of Liv walking around her office, or the streets of Houghton, asking random guys if they'd father her child. His son's sibling. "And if I don't agree to it? If I say no?"

"I would totally understand. It's a big ask, obviously." He snorted, and she smiled. "But I would never hold it against you in any way if you didn't want to do it. I know it would be hard for you to *not* be a part of her life, that you wouldn't be able to not be involved. So if you don't think you can handle it—"

"But what will *you* do if I say no?" A feeling of dread was creeping up his back, and he rolled his tight shoulders, trying to rid himself of it.

"I will still have another child. Or try to, anyway."

"How?" He tried to keep his voice neutral, conversational, not letting his…fear? anger?…be heard. But yeah, it wasn't like he had this conversation every day.

"A sperm bank. I wanted that to be my last option. Just because of the genetic uncertainty. With Kevin, I knew him, his family, everything about him."

"As you do with me," he unnecessarily pointed out.

"Right. And that would be ideal and is why we're even having this conversation."

He held up a hand. "Wait. Is this, like, you're giving me right of first refusal or something?"

She laughed a little. God, it was good to hear that, given how serious the night had turned. "Yeah, I guess that's kind of what I'm doing. You're my first choice, Twain. You were *always* my first choice."

His shoulders eased a little bit. Until she added, "But you're not my *only* choice."

Eight

—◊—

"CAN WE STOP AT ARLENE'S PIZZA?" MATT ASKED, AS HE sat beside her and drove home from Marquette.

Liv had to stop and process what he'd asked, her mind in overload from talking with Twain the night before.

She looked outside, gauging where they were in the two-hour drive from Houghton to Marquette. They'd be driving past Baraga—and the small restaurant with great pizza—in about a half-hour. That'd be just about right for dinnertime. Not that Matty couldn't devour a large sausage pizza any time of the day.

"That sounds good," she said.

"Should you text Dad and see if he, Uncle Sawyer, and Deni want to join us?"

No, she did not want to do that. In fact, it had been hell standing at the ski hill today in the company of Twain. Thank God for Deni, with whom Liv kept company most of the day.

After Liv had explained that she would be having a child with or without Twain's help, he had shaken his head and said it was too much to deal with and that he needed time to wrap his mind around it.

She understood and wanted to give him the space he needed to make his decision.

But she didn't want to have to see him during that time. And especially see how he looked today—bundled up in the cold with a scarf wrapped around his neck, stubble nearly a beard, and his green eyes studying her every time she dared steal a glance at him.

"I think they left the parking area before we did. They're ahead of us," she offered up to her son. "And we don't want to make them sit and wait for us." Easier than telling him that she thought her ovaries might burst into flames if she had to look at Twain over another meal.

Their dinner last night with Sawyer and Deni had reminded her (not that she ever completely forgot) how much she'd not only loved Twain, but also how attracted she'd always been to him. Again, not exactly past tense, but she didn't dwell on that fact.

For a brief moment in her room last night, she'd contemplated not talking to him about the baby and just letting the night lead to what she felt would be a most satisfying conclusion, even if it meant using protection. When he'd put his hands on her hips, she had so badly wanted to lean into his tall body and wrap her arms around his neck.

That was all it would have taken. Twain would have led her from there, as he always had. As she had always wanted it.

But then what? Have the conversation with him about fathering her child afterward? Something about that felt manipulative, which was not her intention. Truly, she didn't want to pressure Twain into doing anything with which he wasn't completely comfortable.

Right of first refusal, he'd called it. Kind of businesslike, but Liv supposed that was how she'd presented it to Twain—a transaction.

With basically no upside for him. Though she would obviously see having another child as a definite plus. And so would Twain, after the fact.

Matty hadn't been planned, and she and Twain had been really young, but Twain adored his son and was a very good father.

She'd laid it out as honestly as she could for him. All she could do now was wait.

And start researching sperm banks.

It wasn't a question that she would proceed with or without

Twain. If anything, Liv felt she was about two years behind the curve.

The two years she'd spent dating Kevin.

No, it was longer than that. When she'd been married to Twain, she'd wanted more children, but the time had never been right.

When she'd been first divorced, she'd toyed with the idea of having a child on her own, but she was still young and had hopes of finding love again with a man who wanted children.

Not having a plentiful crop of single men in their thirties in the Copper Country who were looking for something serious, it had taken a while for Liv to find Kevin.

He'd been interested in her from the first and made all the right noises about wanting to settle down and start a family.

She knew she didn't love him like she'd loved Twain, but after the heartbreak she'd suffered, that notion appealed to her.

But Kevin had only been stringing her along, with no real intentions of marrying her or—and this was worse to Liv—having a child with her.

That point was obvious when she found him in bed with another woman.

And so Liv decided to go ahead and have a child on her own. Her parents would freak, being crazy conservative, but that was fine. They'd freaked when she and Twain had told them she was pregnant and they were getting married, and yet they loved Matty as much as their—many!—other grandchildren.

Besides, with Liv's eldest brother running the restaurant, they were spending the winters in Florida now, so it wasn't as if she'd have to see her mother's disapproving face every day.

And finally having another child would be well worth it.

"Right? Mom?" Matty was saying, and Liv tried to pull her mind away from an image of the cute booties she'd knit. Perhaps she would even add a new line to her business.

"What'd you say, honey? My mind was wandering."

Matty took his eyes from the road to give her a quick look of concern. "You okay?"

She nodded and then pointed to the road, and Matty returned his gaze straight ahead.

"Just thinking about your great performance today," she said. Matty's snort told her he was onto her. "Really. I know you were a little disappointed, but—"

"I could have done better than tenth place," he said, spitting out his finish with derision.

"For a sophomore? Against the top kids from every school in the U.P.? Matty, you have to know that's amazing."

He seemed to think that over, even allowing the "Matty" to slide. "I know you're used to finishing in the top three, or winning, but that is in meets with only two or three schools."

Nothing her son didn't know, but he seemed to puff up a bit behind the wheel as he took in his mother's words.

Her heart ached just looking at him. He would have his father's height, already as tall as the senior boys on the ski team. With Twain's green eyes and dark hair but more of her facial features, he was truly a mix of both his parents.

"Yeah, that's what Heather said, too. That tenth was pretty good for my first time being there."

"I saw that she was there. That was nice of her to drive down for the day when she wasn't even competing. I didn't see her parents there, did I?"

"No. She came with some friends who can drive."

Liv was grateful now that she'd let Matty drive them home from Marquette. She was finding lately she had some of her best conversations with her son when he was behind the wheel. Captive and yet concentrating on something else, so he didn't get all defensive with her. And, of course, he didn't have to look at her, a plus for any teenage boy speaking of anything remotely personal.

"So, is there something more with Heather? More than teammates?"

He shrugged, and Liv thought that maybe his hands tightened

a little on the steering wheel. There was still a little sun left, and the roads were blessedly bare of ice and snow, so Liv didn't worry that asking about his love life would send them into a ditch.

His love life. *Matty's* love life.

How had the time gone so quickly? But it had. And she was more determined than ever to not lose any more time in fulfilling her dream of having another child.

"I guess I thought she was interested in Stevie Robbins," Liv said cautiously.

Another shrug, but this time Liv waited. "I mean, she is... technically. They hang out and stuff, but I don't think it's anything serious. She spends all her time at practice with me."

"Because you're fun to be around," Liv supplied.

"Mom, God," he said. Liv was sure he was rolling his eyes at her compliment.

"You are!" He grunted, and she reached over and tweaked his ear, which he balked at, but a smile came across his sweet face.

A face that—*Oh my God*—had a little bit of stubble on the cheeks.

"Just be careful," Liv said.

"Dad already had *that* talk with me," Matty said, his eyes straight ahead.

"Good," Liv said. Of course, she knew that Twain had talked with Matty about sex and safe sex and wet dreams and all those things. But what Liv was talking about was more than that.

"I know, and make sure you heed your father's advice. But I'm talking about protecting your feelings."

"Geez, Mom."

"I know, I know. Nothing more a fifteen-year-old boy wants to talk about with his mother than his feeeeelings."

A little chuckle from her son, so she went on. "Just be alert, honey. Heather probably loves being around you. Who wouldn't? But you could be just a friend to her. You might be the sounding board she needs when she doesn't want to talk to her girlfriends about Stevie or something. You might be her...safety net."

Silence from him, and Liv feared she'd hit the nail on the head. "And there's nothing wrong with that. You'd be a great friend for anybody, Matt. But…"

"Yeah?"

"It's just… It is so awful when you're the one who loves someone way more than they love you."

They rode in silence until Baraga, neither of them mentioning the fact that they were both perhaps already in that exact situation.

For Liv, she had been since she was eighteen.

Nine

—⁓—

"HOLY WAH," SAWYER SAID RIGHT BEFORE HE SWUNG the axe over his shoulder and split a large log right down the middle.

"You know I've got a wood splitter, right?" Twain said to his brother as he took a seat on a large stump he'd fashioned into a chair, setting Sawyer's mug of coffee on the plastic table next to him and taking a long drag from his own.

"I like the feel of it," Sawyer said, lining up another log on the stump used for wood chopping. "Besides, I needed some fresh air. I like being back in the office—or at least back in the business—but I miss being outside, getting my hands dirty."

They were outside in the back area of the T&B Logging offices. It was warm for this time of year, and Twain knew a thaw—*the* thaw—would soon be upon the Copper Country. Which would put a temporary halt to logging as road restrictions would be put in place, preventing them from hauling their huge equipment from site to site. It usually lasted a couple of weeks, and it gave Twain a chance to get the business' taxes in line, deal with any employee issues that he'd put off, and do any hiring that would be needed. The loggers in his employ usually took off for those weeks, vacationing or heading some place they could log during the duration.

Most of his long-timers came back or even stayed put during the restrictions, but a few of the fly-by-nighters wouldn't return, so Twain liked to have a few possible replacements lined up so they could get right back into the woods as soon as they could start hauling their machinery again.

Sawyer had shown up a couple of hours ago, apparently concerned that Twain had been acting odd two days ago during the ski meet and on the drive back to Hancock with Sawyer and Deni.

Worry. From a man who had basically been a hermit for ten years.

But in the spirit of Sawyer finally rejoining the family and also really needing to talk about this Liv/baby thing, Twain had poured some coffee, handed his big brother an axe, and spilled the whole story.

Two cups—and several chopped logs added to the woodpile— later, Sawyer was still apparently digesting all Twain had told him while working up a healthy sweat.

"Holy wah," he said again, shaking his head. After placing the axe against the stump, he made his way over to Twain, grabbing his coffee and sitting in another stump/chair. "These are cool," he said. "You make 'em?"

Twain nodded. "Yeah. If you have any suggestions, lay them on me." Twain could make anything out of wood, but he knew that his brother—and Deni, for that matter—could design rings around him. He'd been thinking he'd ask Deni for help designing the bar he had in mind for Petey Ryan's place, if that panned out.

"About the chairs or the baby?" Sawyer asked.

Twain laughed. "I meant the chairs, but I guess I'll take whatever you got."

"The chairs are great, don't change a thing." Sawyer took a drink of coffee and stared out past the large garages that housed the feller buncher, log skidder, and the other large equipment, to the forest beyond. "The baby thing?" He shook his head, and Twain was pretty sure he heard another "Holy wah" softly muttered.

"Yeah, I know. Crazy, right? To start all over again at thirty-five?"

Sawyer turned to look at him with a "You're an idiot" look, one he'd perfected when they'd been kids and Twain had wanted to be just like his older brother.

"Fuck you," Sawyer said now, much as he had then, to accompany his look.

"What?"

"I'm forty, and I'm starting over."

Oh. Right. "Yeah, but that's different."

"How?"

"You don't have kids already. You haven't been through it once."

"But it's apples and oranges. You know that, right?"

"No. What?"

"Your relationship with this new kid, this baby, won't be anything like raising Matty. Kids are different. Timing is different. Your relationship with his mother is different."

"Her."

"Her, what?"

Twain shook his head, not believing what he was about to say. "Her. She. We're—Liv is—calling the baby a she."

Sawyer studied him for a second, drinking more coffee. Twain prepared himself for a barrage of abuse for that one. But instead, Sawyer put his cup down, nodded, and continued.

"Okay, she. She will be completely different for you than Matty was. You're not first-timer parents with all of that scariness. You're not trying to stay in school or find a profession. Money's not as big of an issue."

"We're not exactly rolling in it," Twain said, although in the past two days he'd had all the same thoughts Sawyer was now voicing.

Sawyer made an encompassing wave around the buildings of T&B Logging. "It's all yours now, right?"

Twain nodded. "I finished buying Eddie out two years ago. There are still payments on the equipment, of course, and as we modernize more… But yeah, money's okay."

"And Liv still has Matty on her insurance through Tech, right? So presumably the new baby would be covered too?"

Twain nodded and drank more of the strong coffee. He was a shitty coffee maker, but at least it was always frighteningly strong, which his crew needed in the morning and to get through the long, physical days.

"Yes. Matty's covered on Liv's plan. The new baby probably would be too."

His personal health insurance was a bottom-of-the-barrel plan, covering basically nothing except catastrophic events. He had a ton of life insurance, though. He'd made sure of that after his first day of logging with Eddie and seeing how—if you didn't have your wits about you—logging would not be a safe way to make a living. He'd wanted to make sure Liv and Matty were protected.

Still did. Liv was still named a beneficiary on all his stuff.

And now? Would he be adding another name to all of his paperwork? Another child?

After thinking about nothing else since the night in Marquette, Twain had warmed to the idea of having another child. However, he did not like the idea of starting this child's life with already-divorced parents. But would that be better than what Matty had gone through? His life upended at eight years old?

The other option was to try again with Liv. To get back together for the sake of this new child.

He'd be up for that, having genuinely liked being married to Liv. She was always so sweet and supportive. He'd *always* loved their sex life, and his attraction to her had never died. And to come at it now, where they were better emotionally equipped than they had been at nineteen? It actually felt kind of…right to Twain.

And then he remembered that awful night seven years ago. The incredible hurt in Liv's eyes as she threw him out of their apartment. He knew she'd never hear him out on the idea.

The stronger, more self-assured woman she'd become since

they split made it even less of a possibility that she'd set what happened aside and consider the idea of becoming a family again.

Shit, he'd given her so little during their marriage, had absolutely taken her for granted. He'd known how deeply in love she was with him, allowing that emotion while knowing he didn't return it—at least not as deeply as she felt it.

"It's just… I'd like to give her this, you know? As a way of saying… Aw, shit, I don't know."

"Like a belated thank-you parting gift?" Sawyer said. While Twain had been thinking about a family reunion that wouldn't—couldn't—happen, Sawyer had stood up and now had the stump chair tipped over, examining the legs and back. The engineer geek was always looking at stuff, seeing how it was made.

"Yeah, kind of, I guess. Is that fucked up?" Twain asked his older brother. Not that Sawyer could give great advice on rational behavior after basically going AWOL when Molly died.

Sawyer shrugged, placing the chair back to its normal position, nodding at the chair as he did so, like he approved. Twain silently preened, liking the approval from a stickler such as Sawyer.

Sawyer looked at him, hands on his hips, and shrugged. "What? I'm the one who's going to give you advice on what's fucked up or not? The whole thing seems a bit messed up, but I do know how much Liv's always wanted more children."

"You have? How? Wait…more *children*? Like, plural?"

Sawyer chuckled, turning out toward the woods again. Twain loved being in the forest all day—it energized him while also bringing a Zen kind of peace to him. It looked like that trait was also in Sawyer by the way he was wistfully looking at the woods. Twain absently wondered if their younger brother, Huck, also shared that affinity with the woodlands. They had as kids together, but lately he wasn't sure where Huck's head was at.

Until he remembered what Sawyer had just said about Liv always wanting more kids.

"I'm thinking she's probably given up on the plural part by

now. But yeah, she'd talk about more kids when you guys were married. Not at first—I'm guessing because things were so tight—but around the time you and Eddie made your deal and Matty started school."

"And she told *you* this?" Twain was thrown for a loop with that one. Yes, Liv had mentioned perhaps having another child once or twice to Twain—or had it been more often than that? But to talk about it with his brother?

"Once, maybe, when I happened to be in the room. But no, this was to Molly. They were pretty close there for a couple of years before…"

Before Molly had died in a car accident. An accident that Twain knew Sawyer still anguished over, because he wasn't so sure it was an accident at all.

"You two were awfully good to us in those days. I don't know if I ever properly thanked you. But the meals, Molly taking Matty every now and then…" Sawyer turned from his forest view and looked down at Twain where he still sat in his chair. "Thank you," Twain said to his brother.

Sawyer snorted and made a dismissive wave. "Oh, please. You've paid whatever you thought you owed us—me—back a thousand times over."

At Twain's skeptical look, Sawyer sat back down in his chair, faced him, and said, "If you hadn't gotten me to see Alison Jukuri, if you hadn't gotten me Lucy, if you hadn't helped me with the Ice Cube—which I consider almost as good therapy as Alison gave me—I don't know what… I'm not sure I'd even be here, Twain. And I know I sure as hell wouldn't have been in any shape to be what Deni needs. Not to mention the help you gave me with her."

Uncomfortable with Sawyer's brutal honesty and not wanting to revisit that dark time in his brother's life because it still hurt, Twain said, "Where is Lucy, anyway? I wouldn't have thought you would come out to the land of trees and not bring her."

A look of happiness came over his brother's face. A look Twain had seen more in the past two months than he had in the last ten years combined.

"She won't leave Deni when we're at the office. We have a damn Lands' End dog bed set up for her in my spacious office, but whenever we're there, Lucy goes and hangs out in Deni's cramped cubicle. She wouldn't even come with me today since Deni wasn't coming."

Twain sat back, smiling, picturing his brother's dog and his girlfriend bonding together and ignoring Sawyer. "Earlier you said you were starting over at forty." Sawyer nodded. "Are you talking about kids too? Or just, you know, Deni?"

"Kids too," Sawyer said. "Deni wants them, and though I didn't think they were in the cards for me after Molly…I find I really want them. With Deni."

"You've talked about this? Even though you've been together, what, three months?"

Sawyer shrugged. "Yeah, in abstract ways right now. But I know she's the one. And she knows it. I just don't want her to freak out by going too fast. Hell, I'm just trying to get her to commit to the same house first."

"Seems like she's committed."

"She is. She's just being cautious."

"Because of her SAD? Or because you were an asshole when you found out about it?"

Sawyer shot him a dirty look, but then sighed and admitted, "Both, I suppose. I don't blame her, but she knows I'm not going anywhere. I can wait. But then, she's only twenty-eight. We've got lots of time."

"Whereas Liv and I don't."

"You still have time, just not as much. But I'd say if you are going to be a part of this, you'd better jump on the bandwagon now, because from what you've said, she is going ahead with or without you."

"Yeah," Twain said. That odd feeling he'd had ever since Saturday night crept up on him again. He hadn't been able to define it completely, but it was unease mixed with…something.

"Molly and I used to talk about how lucky, in a way, you and Liv were to have had Matty when you were so young. We'd say you'd have it all done by the time you were forty and be able to relax and enjoy life."

Twain snorted at that. "You're never done."

Sawyer sported a small, sad smile. "Yeah, I've come to realize that." He put his big hand on Twain's knee, squeezed, and then removed it to take his cup in hand. "You had Matt young. Molly and I wanted to wait until we had the business off the ground. Then Molly got…sick.

"I guess what I'm trying to say is, you don't know what's going to happen. You can have a plan"—he motioned to Twain—"like playing hockey at Tech and getting a great degree, maybe even getting a shot at the NHL." He put his cup down and leaned forward, resting his forearms on his thighs. "Or marrying the woman you love, building a business together, and having a houseful of children." His head dipped a little bit, but Twain resisted the urge to put a hand on his brother's shoulder. Sawyer could work through it on his own. "And it can all turn to shit. Or so you think at the time. But sometimes that shit slowly turns into the greatest gift of your life. Like a son you adore or a second chance at love with someone you absolutely cannot believe loves you as much as you do her."

Twain felt a lump in his throat, knowing just how true Sawyer's words were.

Sawyer sat up and turned to Twain. "I guess the main thing is, do you *want* another child?"

The question Twain had thought about nonstop the past few days. And, if he was honest with himself, had thought about numerous times before when wondering what life would bring him after he and Liv split.

Matty was his joy, his life, and he loved being a father. Spending time together in the forest, just the two of them, was the greatest gift Twain had ever been given. And to have that again? Not to replace Matty, as he'd wondered if Liv was doing. But to feel that kind of deep, unconditional love with another human being? A human being who was his?

The work involved, the diapers, the potty training? Yeah, all that stuff sucked, but there had also been a lot of bonding and growing together that had happened at that stage. The joy of first steps, first time going to the bathroom on their own, all of that. Most of those things he'd missed with Matty because he'd been in the forest from dawn to dusk, trying to get a foothold on a living for his family. And he'd probably miss those milestones again, but Liv would tell him about them with a gleam of love in her eyes, imparting every detail, just like she had with Matty.

"Yes," he said to Sawyer. "I want another child." Sawyer only nodded, as if he had known that would be Twain's answer all along.

Hell, maybe Twain had known, too.

"So then, all the points Liv made to you about the practicality of it being with the same partner are just as true for you. It would be a full sibling to Matt." At Twain's quirked eyebrow, Sawyer amended, "*She* would be a part of a home that has already figured out how to do custody and child support and making joint decisions, all of that."

Twain was nodding when Sawyer added, "Unless there's someone else you could see being the mother of your child?"

With a grin, Twain said, "You said Deni wanted kids?"

Sawyer's eyes turned deadly. "Fuck you. Don't even joke like that."

Twain held his hands up in surrender. "Relax. I'm just kidding."

"Not funny."

"I'm getting that," Twain said. "But the answer is no. I don't see any other woman than Liv being the mother of my child. Deni included."

Sawyer nodded, again knowing the answer to the question before he posed it. "Now, for the kicker. Could you see anybody else being the father of Liv's child?"

Jealousy. That was the other emotion that had paired with uncertainty, circulating through his system since Sunday.

"No," he said in what came out as some sort of primordial grunt.

Sawyer grinned, stood, and ruffled Twain's hair as he'd done so many times when they were kids.

"I think we're done here," he said as he walked away.

Ten

—∽∽—

"THANKS FOR COMING HERE," LIV SAID TO TWAIN AS HE came into her house. She motioned him to the kitchen after she took his big logging coat and hung it up in the hall closet.

"Seems like a conversation to have in private," he said.

"How about some coffee?" she asked him. He was running his hands through his hair, and even though he'd obviously tried to clean up after work, a halo of sawdust rose from his head, caught in the overhead light of the kitchen.

The familiar sight made Liv's heart clench for a second. They hadn't lived in this home when they'd been married, but seeing dust fly from him nightly was a strong memory. Watching from the hallway, she wasn't close enough to smell him, but she swore she could detect the mixture of wood, fuel, and the outdoors.

He still had on the thick pants that he logged in, designed for safety and warmth. The thermal undershirt, the rough cotton work shirt, and the suspenders that held the saw patch on his shoulder in place all brought back numerous memories of her peeling those clothes from him and leading him into the shower to let the steaming hot water pour over him, easing his sore muscles.

She'd inevitably join him in the shower and ease him in other ways.

And he always...eased her. Every time.

But there would be no *easing* tonight. And from the tone of his voice when he'd called her and said he wanted to "talk," Liv guessed there would probably be no easing for procreation reasons in the future.

"Coffee would be great, thanks," he said, sitting at her kitchen table. It was an old oak table that Twain had found at an estate sale and refurbished for them. In their small apartment, it had fit perfectly with all of the leaves removed. Here in her house, she'd put only one of the three leaves in. That was enough for just Matty and her.

How many times had she wished to have more children and have to use all of the leaves on the table?

Shaking the thought from her head, she started a pot of coffee and then turned to Twain, who was running his hands along the wood. Remembering their times as a family spent at the table? Or just wondering if it needed to be refinished?

"Have you eaten? Matty and I had lasagna. There's a lot left over."

"I don't want to be any trouble," he said, which she took as a yes.

"No trouble. It'll just be a minute to nuke it."

"You don't need to wait on me, Liv," he said as he started to rise from the table.

She waved him back down. "It's fine, really. Besides, you don't know where anything is."

She could feel his eyes on her as she took the Pyrex pan from the fridge, cut a generous slice of lasagna, placed it on a plate, and put it in the microwave. She grabbed a mug from the cupboard, brought it to the table, and placed it in front of him. She added some of the leftover garlic bread to the plate of lasagna for the last twenty seconds of cooking time. When it was ready, so was the coffee. She poured him a mugful, put the carafe back on the burner, and sat down to join him at the table.

"Do you want to talk first?" Twain said to her while he hungrily eyed the plate before him.

She motioned to the food. "Go ahead while it's warm. Matty won't be home until eleven. We have plenty of time." At the look of shock on Twain's face, she quickly added, "To talk. Plenty of time to talk."

He swallowed hard, his strong neck vibrating with the motion, and then picked up his fork and started eating.

She pulled her ever-present knitting over to her from the other end of the table where she'd laid it earlier, and began to knit quietly while Twain ate.

"This is great, thanks," he said between bites.

"No problem."

He motioned to her knitting. "Looks good. Go Copper Kings."

Smiling, she said, "It's for Megan's graduation. I thought I'd get an early start." She was making her niece a scarf in Calumet colors—navy and silver.

"Megan's graduating? Wow. Yeah, I guess she was a couple of years older than Matt."

Megan was Liv's youngest niece, by several years. All of her older brothers and sisters had finished having children—and they'd had a lot—by the time Liv had been in middle school. Her younger brother, Joe, was still single and childless at thirty-three, an anomaly in her family. Megan had been a surprise baby for Liv's sister Barb but had been a nice cousin playmate for Matty.

"Actually," Twain said, wiping his mouth on a napkin, "that kind of leads us to one of the questions I have." He looked at her steadily and added, "And I have many."

A brief fluttering of hope unfurled inside Liv. He wouldn't need to ask questions if he'd already decided to say no, right?

"Okay," she said tentatively, afraid to let her hope show.

He nodded. "What is your family going to say about this? Generally, you having a baby on your own, not married. Specifically, with me as the father."

She relaxed in her chair. These questions she could answer—she'd been thinking about them for years. With Kevin, she'd put them on the back burner, thinking they wouldn't come up, or at least they'd be answered in the context of their relationship.

But there was no relationship with Kevin anymore, and she'd recently mentally recalled the perfectly honed thoughts and answers she'd previously had.

"I've thought about that, of course," she said, setting down her knitting and looking at Twain.

He didn't seem surprised at that declaration and waved for her to go on while he scooped up another forkful of lasagna.

"They'll let their disapproval be known, of course. I'm prepared for that. But my mom knows how badly I wanted more children." His fork paused briefly mid-shovel, but she went on. "And I think they'll come around eventually. At the end of the day, they'll love this baby like they do all their grandchildren.

"I'm thirty-five years old; it's not like I need their permission or anything. I know they'll be hurt at first, but…" She shrugged. Her parents were ultra-conservative, and she'd hurt them badly by becoming pregnant and unmarried at nineteen, but they adored Matty. "The upside is they spend the winters in Florida now, so even if they're full of disapproval, I'll only have to see it six months out of the year."

Twain gave a little snort of laughter. "Good for you. I know how much it hurt you when they didn't…understand with Matty."

He knew that? She'd tried to hide from Twain the tears she'd shed over her parents' disappointment in her.

"I expect it will be the same this time at first, but I'm not nineteen, and I don't hang much on my parents' approval anymore."

He nodded, as if liking her choice. She certainly did. It was liberating and had been hard-fought, but somewhere along the line, a few years after divorcing Twain, she'd found the strength (or maybe the exhaustion!) to let that all go.

"And when they—and everybody else, for that matter—find out she's *my* baby?"

"Well, I have some thoughts, but that's something we would decide together."

"What are your thoughts?" He had polished off the lasagna

and bread by now, and she motioned to the plate in a "More?" way, but he waved her off and placed his napkin on the empty plate. He moved it to the side and slid his mug in front of him, holding it with both hands, his green eyes intent on her, giving her all of his attention.

"Before I go into all that, you are seriously considering this, right? I'm not just talking in hypotheticals?"

He sat back in his chair, his big hands still wrapped around his mug, eyes still boring into hers. "I'm seriously considering this, yes. This isn't a negotiation, Liv. It's me trying to figure out a way to make it actually work."

She could feel her eyes fill with tears, and she tried desperately to blink them back. But no, the drops fell heavily onto her cheeks, and she quickly brushed them away. "I'm sorry," she said. "I swore to myself when you called that I wouldn't cry in front of you, no matter which way this went."

He leaned forward, his elbows on the table. He put the mug down, and it seemed for a second as if he were going to slide his hand across the table and reach for her. But he didn't. He just flattened his palms on the oak and let out a small sigh. "You can cry in front of me, Liv. You always could, you know. Even if you didn't."

She did know. At least, she'd figured that out after the fact. She'd been so afraid of being...too much for Twain when they'd been first married. He'd liked her because what they had was light and fun, and she was afraid to be anything more than that in front of him. So the worries and insecurities of being a young mother and wife were feelings she kept carefully hidden from her husband.

But he was right. She could cry in front of the man. He would never hold something so honest against her.

If only she'd figured that out sooner, perhaps—

No. She'd beaten herself up enough after the divorce with the "what-ifs" of their life. She was beyond that now.

She wiped her tears on the sleeve of her sweater and nodded

at Twain. "I know. Thanks."

He relaxed a little, sitting back in his seat. "So, your thoughts on what we'll tell people?"

She nodded, clearing her throat, determined to get through this without becoming a puddle of joy in front of Twain. Besides, he hadn't actually said yes, yet.

"If you meant what you said in Marquette—and I'm not holding you to that—about wanting to be involved in her life, and not just a sperm donor—"

"I meant it. I would be as much a father to her as I am to Matt. In every way, including financially." That issue obviously settled in his mind, he waved her on.

"Okay. Well, I think we just let it be known that we wanted another child, but not to get back together. I even think we could get some of the town's more...*vocal* people on our side to get the word out with our own version."

"Spin it the way we want to the biggest gossips," he said, and she nodded. "But you know there will still be talk. People will think we were just sleeping together and had another unplanned pregnancy."

"Of course. And they'll say I was just trying to get you back."

"After the way our marriage ended, I doubt people will think that."

She shrugged. Maybe not. "The point is, we can tell a few people the truth and then let the chips fall where they may. You and I, better than most, know what this town can do with a juicy rumor."

"Yeah," he said then sighed and shook his head. "We certainly do.

"Okay, I'm with you on that one—let 'em think what they want. We'll tell the people who matter to us the truth, and the rest can go fuck themselves."

"Right," she said. "As long as Matt doesn't get hit in the crossfire."

"Exactly. Which brings up the biggest question on my list.

What about Matt?"

"Of course. He's obviously my biggest concern too."

"Did you ever talk to him about having another baby when you were…with Kevin?" He practically growled Kevin's name, and Liv found she liked that. Childish, sure, but Twain had never been jealous, and not that he was now, but… It just made her feel good, that was all.

"No. I didn't talk to Matty about it because I was never really…sure about Kevin. He never moved in or anything. I would have told you if we were thinking about living together or anything more serious."

"Thank you."

She nodded. "Of course. So, I propose that we not say anything to Matty until I'm actually pregnant. Who knows? I might have missed my window completely."

"Thirty-five is still plenty young, Liv."

She nodded. "I know. But you just never know with this kind of thing. If it doesn't happen, I don't even want him knowing we were trying."

He rubbed a hand along his stubble, which to Liv's guess was on about day four. In fact, it had carried over from stubble to the light beard category. Every phase looked good on Twain.

"And if…*when* we're pregnant?" he asked.

The use of "when" was great, but his use of "we're" was even more of an indication to Liv of Twain's commitment to her dream.

"Then we sit him down—together—and tell him the truth. That I wanted another child and because we'd created such a great kid together once, I asked you to be the father. And that he's going to be an amazing big brother."

"Think it will be that easy?"

She shrugged. "Is *anything* easy with a teenager? It will all come down to how it affects his life, and the truth is, probably not that much. The baby would be born, at the earliest, halfway through his junior year. He's hardly home now between skiing, friends, and working with you. Add to that the ability to drive, girls…" Her throat constricted at the last, thinking about Matt's crush on Heather Summers. Liv was convinced her baby was going to have his heart broken and had tried to warn him, but…

"Okay. So, we're shooting down any questions about us getting back together?" There was question in his voice. A tone that puzzled Liv.

"Yes. Of course. Right?"

"Right, right. I just wanted to be sure. I mean…"

The tears didn't come this time, but there was just as much emotional turbulence wafting through Liv. Hope and love, quickly washed away by memories of betrayal and hurt. Oh, the gut-wrenching hurt she'd felt that awful night. And the days and weeks that followed.

"Yes. We just tell the truth. Let the chips fall where they may."

There was a long moment of silence with Twain's green eyes searching hers before he slowly nodded his agreement.

The old Liv would have questioned that delay, would have hung on to it and blown it into some big, hopeful dream.

But that Liv had grown up and become a woman who made her own dreams come true.

Like she was now.

"Okay," she said. "What else?"

"Hmmm?"

"Your other questions?"

"Oh, right. Umm, I guess we covered the main things. If you're willing to let me be a part of her life, let me help out financially, see her as much as I see Matt. Though at first, with nursing and all, I realize it will be different. So…"

"Yes?" she whispered, too afraid to say more lest she tip the scale in the other direction.

"Then I would love to have a child with you, Liv Beck."

"Really?" She gasped, the tears flowing freely now. She didn't even try to hold them back. Twain was right—she could cry in front of him. He moved to get up, probably to comfort her, but she motioned for him to stay seated. "It's okay," she said. "I'm okay. Just very happy. Thank you, Twain. Thank you so much."

"You're welcome, Liv," he said quietly, then he smiled. Not the playful grin that had her saying yes to the back seat on the first night they'd been together. This was a smile of joy, the one he'd had when he'd first held Matty in his arms. "I feel like I should be the one saying thank you. You gave me such a gift in Matt, Liv. That you want me to be the father of your child, after everything that we've gone through…" His voice roughened, and he cleared his throat but didn't go on. Still, she knew how he felt. They'd created something of love and joy together in Matty, and now they would do it again.

"So," she said when she was able to speak again. "I've done some looking into artificial insemination in the area. We could have it done here, or we could go to Marquette. My insurance will cover some of it, but not all. But I have some money from my knitting put away for—"

"You're thinking what? That I jack off into some cup and then they put me inside you with a turkey baster or something?"

"Well, I think it's a little more substantial than a turkey baster, but basically, yes."

"And that's the route you want to go? Doctors? Sterile environments? Added expenses when we'll have a new baby on the way?"

Every nerve in her body screamed "no," but she'd asked so much of him already, she didn't want to ask for that too, even if she'd…what? She'd love having sex with Twain again? Could she? Better question: could she make love with Twain Beck and walk away from his bed without reverting to the lovesick schoolgirl she'd been?

He reached across the wide table. Even with his long arms, he couldn't reach her hands where they sat on the edge of the table. She would have to meet him halfway.

Slowly she moved her hands across the worn wood until they were beside his.

He placed his heavy hands on top of hers. "No matter what we went through, no matter how it all ended." He waited, then squeezed, causing her to look up from their laced hands and into his warm green eyes. "I never stopped *wanting* you, Liv."

It wasn't exactly the word she wanted to hear, but what he said still warmed her like submerging in hot bathwater on a January day.

"Don't you think we should create this baby just like we did Matty?"

"I...I..."

He'd been caressing her palm with his thumb but now stilled. "Unless you don't want to. I'll understand if it's too hard for you. I don't want to—"

"No. It's not too hard for me," she lied. "It would certainly be more convenient and less expensive." But complicated. Much more complicated.

"And a hell of a lot more fun," he said, the grin now in full force.

She'd never been able to resist that grin. There was no reason to think that she could now. Not when he was trying to talk her into doing something she desperately wanted to do anyway.

She slid her hand out from under his, then turned it to his other one, creating a handshake. "Deal," she said, smiling at him, saying so much more to him than just the one word.

"Deal," he said, as they shook hands.

And just like that, Liv had what she'd wanted for so long, or at least the promise of it.

And also just like that, because it never seemed completely underground, the Pet Rock she'd gotten off her shoulder so long ago seemed to be raising its moss-covered head.

Eleven

—⚬—

"THIS IS REALLY NICE, TWAIN," SHE SAID TO HIM A WEEK
after he'd been in her kitchen and they'd decided to make a baby.

"You sound surprised," he said, though there was no
defensiveness in his voice, more of a playfulness.

Good, because they'd need every playful note they had in
their arsenal to get through this night—their first together in over
seven years.

"I guess I do, don't I," she admitted. "No offense. I just didn't
know what to picture." She continued to look around his small
home in Calumet. She'd driven by it a thousand times since Twain
had purchased it five years ago after living in an apartment the
first couple of years after they split. And of course she'd dropped
off and picked up Matty many times, but she always stayed in the
car, Twain coming out to talk with her as they made the Matty
exchange.

It was much larger than her home in Houghton, but Liv
imagined it cost much less being in Calumet and from what it
had looked like—at least from the outside—when he'd bought it.

And she could tell now how much work Twain had done to
the place. The wood details were all Twain, some of them even
being the same as ones he had incorporated into the design of her
house. The furniture was big, oversized, and comfortable looking,
like Twain himself. Neutral colors, with several of the throws she'd
knitted and given him and Matty over the years strewn across the

back of the couch, the chairs, and a big ottoman. Matty's gaming devices and the television took up nearly a full wall of the living room. The kitchen was small, but functional. Twain wasn't much of a cook, but Matty came back to her place always well fed, and every once in a while he would comment on a new recipe Twain had tried out for the two of them.

The dining room table was littered on one end with piles of paper, an adding machine, and a laptop. But the other end was clear, save two cloth placemats in a red and khaki stripe. It was similar to Liv's table, except with her knitting replacing his paperwork. She kept all those things pertaining to her knitting business in the spare bedroom, which she'd been using as an office.

Hopefully soon, she'd be making an office area in the basement and turning that room into a nursery.

Twain's home suited him and had his personality, but it definitely lacked a woman's touch. Which made Liv happy in a perverse way.

"Would it be okay if I saw Matty's room, do you think?" she asked. She'd gathered scraps of information from the things Matty had said about his room at his father's, but Liv had not been able to piece them together for a complete picture of where her son spent half his time.

"Of course," he said, waving her to the stairway.

They'd chosen tonight as their first (and last?) attempt because Matty was at an overnight at Justin Porter's. Liv had asked if Twain would be okay with her coming to his house in Calumet instead of them meeting at her place.

She knew how hard this would be on her—to make love with Twain. She didn't want to have the added emotional attachment of it being in her home. In her bed. She wanted to be able to leave right after, walk out his door, and not look back until they knew if a repeat performance would be needed.

And, okay, so she'd probably sob the entire drive home from Calumet to Houghton, but at least it would be in her car and not in her bed.

It was one of the homes built during the mining boom. Not one of the tiny dwellings that sat close together and right by the road (less shoveling), but also not one of the mansions in neighboring Laurium that had belonged to the copper mine owners once upon a time.

She'd loved those houses as a kid, imagining the balls and soirees that must have happened during the copper mining heyday of the early nineteen hundreds.

The mining industry had brought great wealth to the area generations ago, but it also left a sad legacy. She'd also grown up with the arch at the Italian Hall memorializing the seventy-three lives lost during a fire in the disaster of 1913, which was brought on by a struggle between owners and striking workers.

She could feel Twain's eyes on her backside as she climbed the narrow stairs in front of him, and she tried to concentrate on the house instead of what was about to happen.

Her hand ran along the beautiful bannister, which looked new, but blended in well with the history of the house. "You've been busy," she said quietly, more to herself than to him. All those nights when she'd wondered what Twain was doing—or more importantly, *who* Twain was doing—and he'd probably been working on his home.

"I have. I took my time with it after I got Matt's room livable. Sawyer would help me some, and I'd help him on a place he built past Copper Harbor. So, yeah, almost five years when I had the time."

She looked over her shoulder at him and smiled. "And when did you ever have time?" The business kept Twain in the woods for incredibly long hours, but Liv knew he loved what he did for a living. She had envied that, until Molly had talked her into selling her knitted mittens at an arts and crafts show years ago. She now got the same satisfaction from the happiness her small creations brought people as Twain seemed to get from being in the woods all day.

But it had taken her a while to get there.

"Exactly. But I finally got the last of the renovations done around last Thanksgiving."

Probably when she'd taken Matty to her parents' in Florida for the holiday. It had been a hard decision—not sharing Matty during the holidays for the first time—but Twain had been gracious and had wished them a good trip.

While she'd been eating her mother's famous dressing with the air conditioner blasting, Liv had visions of Twain snowshoeing his way into whatever cave Sawyer was probably living in, and the two of them sharing a can of beans in front of an open fire as they sat shivering in the cold.

But no, apparently he was putting the finishing touches on the home he'd created for her son.

"But now, I'll need to start over," Twain said as he indicated the first room on the second floor. He reached in front of her, brushing his arm against her, causing Liv to jump just a tiny bit. Pushing the door open, he waved to the room that currently housed Twain's tools, a couple of sealed paint cans, and several sawhorses. "I'll get this cleared out before the baby comes. Haven't ever bought pink paint before, but I don't think I'll have to hand in my man card to do it."

She laughed. "We don't *know* it will be a girl," she said. There was no guarantee she'd even get pregnant, but she chose not to voice that particular concern. "Hold off on paint colors until… we know for sure."

"Do you want to find out the gender…if…when?"

They had chosen not to find out with Matty, wanting the surprise. Not that the existence of Matty when they'd thought they were being careful wasn't surprise enough. But Liv found herself nodding at Twain. "Yes, I think I'd like to know this time. But if you don't want to…" In the past, Liv would have tried to read Twain's mind on what he wanted and matched her wishes accordingly. But now she just finished with, "Then I'll make sure the doctor only tells me, and I promise I won't let it slip."

"A pink room at your house wouldn't give it away?" he joked.

Neither of them mentioned that it would be unlikely for Twain to ever see the nursery at her house.

"I'm thinking yellow," she said.

"I'm thinking I'd like to know this time, too," he said. She smiled to herself as he led her down the hallway and opened the door to what was clearly Matty's room, if you went by the poster of someone skiing off a cliff.

Walking into the room felt so odd to her. It *felt* like Matty right away, and yet it was foreign to her that her son, her baby, spent so much time in a room she'd never before seen.

Even in school, she'd toured his classroom during conferences and had seen his desk and his artwork on the walls.

She walked slowly into the room, as if she could be caught trespassing at any moment. Seeming to know the strange feelings she was experiencing, Twain laid a hand on her shoulder. She should move forward or take his hand away, but she found she liked the comfort it brought her. She'd been anxiety ridden since the night Twain had said yes to a baby at her house last week. And today she couldn't get any work done, her concentration being shredded with thoughts of what was to come that evening.

Standing in the middle of her son's second home with Twain's big, warm hand on her shoulder should have sent her into overdrive, but she found herself starting to relax.

Like most of these older homes, the rooms were small, but Twain had done some creative built-ins, creating a headboard for the queen bed that in essence took up the whole wall. It had shelves and random crevices, each jam-packed with the things Matty constantly accumulated. On both ends, the last vertical shelf divider was made up of welded-together ski poles, creating one long cubby.

"That's great," she said, pointing to the entire wall.

"Thanks," Twain said. With gentle pressure from his hand, he turned her around so she saw the wall that faced the bed.

"Oh my God," Liv said as she took in the display above a chest of drawers just like one Twain had built for their apartment.

No, it was more than a display, she saw as she moved closer. It was almost a custom-made paneling that covered the entire wall. Mounted to the wall was a collection of antique wooden skis, sans bindings, in various colors and sizes arranged in a staggered, subway tile kind of way. It looked effortless, but Liv knew it must have taken a very long time to get skis the right lengths and widths to make it all match up. From what she could see, none had been cut off.

Mounted in the middle of the skis, above the dresser, was a small television. At various areas of the skis, where there was a tiny gap, were the webbed tips of ski poles that extended as pegs. Matty had thrown towels and clothes over some of them, but many were still bare.

"That is so cool," she said.

"Thanks. Sawyer had the idea—I can't take credit for that. He helped me put it together, but Matt and I found most of the skis togehter, at garage sales and stuff. One guy we did a logging job with had a bunch of them just gathering dust in his garage. I offered to buy them from him, but he was just happy to get rid of them."

Liv wondered why Matty had never told her about this wonderful room Twain had created for him. Did he think it would have hurt Liv to know about it?

Would he have been right?

More likely, he was just a kid with an out-of-sight-out-of-mind mentality when it came to things like interior decorating.

She examined the ski wall more closely while Twain stepped away from her and leaned against one of the side walls, watching her. She could feel the heat of his gaze on her back. Well, backside was more likely.

She moved to the top of Matty's dresser, picking up all the things he'd dropped on the piece of furniture. A movie ticket stub; a pack of gum. Just like he did at home.

Home. Not her home. But this was Matty's home too.

"You know," Twain said, his voice gruff. He cleared his throat and continued as Liv stayed where she was, her back to him. "It never occurred to me that you hadn't seen Matt's room. That you'd want to. But of course you would."

She nodded, gaining her thoughts. "I mean, I asked Matty about it, of course. But you know…"

"He's a boy," Twain finished for her.

"Right." She turned, facing him. His arms were folded over his chest, and his big body seemed to suck the air out of the small room.

The reason she was even at Twain's house swept over her, and she felt a flush creep over her. A smile graced Twain's rugged face. She never could hide anything from him.

Trying to get back to her previous train of thought (and perhaps stalling just a teensy bit), she waved a hand, encompassing the room. "It's really great, Twain. I'm sure he loves it."

Twain shrugged and stepped away from the wall. "Who knows. Like I said, he's a boy. And now a teenager at that. But we had some fun finding the skis and putting the wall together."

A strong feeling that she couldn't name threatened to overwhelm Liv, and she stepped over to the platform bed and lowered herself onto it.

"Liv?" Twain said, then moved to the bed, squatting on his haunches to face her. "You okay?"

"It's weird, right?" she said. "I know Matty spends half his time here with you. And we talk about what you and he do together. I know you're a great father, Twain." She looked up from her folded hands to meet that green gaze, which was looking at her with compassion. And a little confusion.

She shook her head softly. "I mean, obviously. That's why I'm here—because you're the father I want for my baby." He reached out, taking her hands in his, but waiting for her to continue.

In the old days, she would have stopped. Wouldn't have wanted to spill her feelings to Twain, to bore him.

But he was always willing to listen to her. How many times had he been like he was right now: poised and waiting to hear her opinion, to hear how she felt.

And she'd been afraid to show him. Had waved her feelings away with an "It's nothing" because she was... What? Oh yeah, Pet Rock. She was afraid she'd lose him.

Somewhere in the back of her mind, she knew she'd done herself a disservice by not speaking up, by not sharing with him. By letting fear rule her.

And she'd worked through that, had let go of her fears. After all, she'd survived her worst fear—that she would lose Twain.

But now, she realized how unfair she'd been to Twain, too. To not tell him when she was scared, or sad, or...anything.

Squaring her shoulders and turning her hands to lace her fingers with his, she tried to explain how she was feeling being in Matty's second home.

"I worry when Matty's not with me, like any parent does. But I do know how safe he is with you, Twain. My God, just from being a logger, you're one of the most safety-conscious people I know." He squeezed her hands but stayed silent.

"And there are times, believe me, when I am more than happy that Matty is with you and I have a chance to think."

"Yeah, from about eight to twelve years old, when it was all poop and booger humor," he said, and she laughed.

She looked around the room again and didn't even try to stop the tears that formed at the corners of her eyes. "But I always knew he was in good hands with you, Twain. Great hands. Do you know what a relief that is for a mother? To know her son is happy. That he loves being with his father. That he's taken care of, paid attention to." Not wanting to let go of his hands, she motioned with her chin to the room as a whole. "To know that he's as cherished when he's away from me as he is when he's with me. That his father cares enough to create—and I'm sure it wasn't easy—such a safe and meaningful oasis."

"Of course I do, Liv," he said, confusion in his eyes. God bless him, it would never occur to him that many women didn't have the kind of care for their child that Twain gave Matty. Several of her coworkers, in fact, came in every other Monday with tales of their ex-husband's poor childcare skills. They'd be frantic the Fridays before they had to hand their children over, knowing they wouldn't get a balanced meal (or sometimes *any* meal) or good sleep until the kids were dropped off on Sunday night.

"You gave me the gift of Matty fifteen years ago. But the way you've raised and loved him, always, but in particular after the divorce, has been the best gift you could have given me, Twain." She saw him swallow, his Adam's apple bobbing in his strong neck. "Thank you for that," she whispered.

It seemed so natural, so right, to lean forward and gently kiss his lips. She felt a tear break free and roll down her cheek, resting first on her mouth and then transferring to his full lips as she leaned back.

"Liv," he whispered, "let's make another gift." His tongue flicked out and tasted her tear, pulling it from his lush lower lip into his mouth.

A mouth that Liv wanted to devour. The soft kiss of thanks she'd given him was not nearly enough. And really, that's why she was here, wasn't it? A good, hopefully baby-creating devouring.

No. No, she couldn't devour him for the simple reason that she wanted to so badly. Because although she was here for baby making, and she had every intention of enjoying the process, she knew she needed to protect her feelings. Needed this to be all about the physical and not dredge up her ages-old love of Twain Beck.

There would be no more kisses—devouring or otherwise. At least not on the lips.

She closed her eyes, stayed close to him, and waited, as she always had, for Twain to take it to the next level, to make the first move.

But he didn't. She opened her eyes and saw him staring at her with the same heat that she felt. "It's your party, Liv," he whispered while his gaze dipped to her mouth. "I'm just the invited guest."

Yes, this time would be completely different from all the

times before. There would be no long, soul-crushing kisses. And now she would make the first move. And second. And third. Being in control would help her protect herself from him.

She let go of his hands and ran hers up his arms, the feel of his soft, well-worn flannel shirt not concealing the strength and brawn just beneath.

Feeling the muscles ripple underneath flooded glorious memories through Liv's brain. Hearing the hitch in Twain's breath as she brushed a hand at the base of his neck where the flannel shirt ended and his thermal Henley started gave her whatever courage she needed.

"Then let's get this party started," she said, winking at him. And while he tried to recover from his apparent shock, she slid from the platform bed to kneel in front of him and wrapped her arms around him.

Twelve

—⚋—

THE PAST TWO WEEKS—EVER SINCE LIV DROPPED HER bombshell in that Marquette hotel room—had been a surreal blur for Twain.

But that was nothing compared to the confusing reaction he was having to Liv's little body melting against his.

Part of him reverted to just being a guy with a woman in his arms. Soft. Warm. Good. (Thought to himself, with the requisite caveman grunts.)

Another part desperately tried to wipe away thoughts that this sexy woman who was wrapping her arms around his neck was the same woman he'd hurt so deeply. The woman who he'd never wanted to hurt.

Liv.

And that was the part that won—the part of himself that had always been attracted to Liv, ever since that first night. He'd found such comfort and solace in her body. His fears about being a young father and husband had quieted when he'd been inside her, staring into her blue eyes. Eyes that had never been able to hide how much she loved him, no matter how hard she'd tried.

The eyes that were taking him in now, studying his face as she leaned back away from him.

A questioning look crossed her face, but Twain didn't know the answer she was looking for—didn't even understand the question.

It was just like it had always been: Liv needing more than he could give her, or him not even knowing what it was she needed because she was too afraid of losing him to let him see.

His feelings of failure as a husband rushed through him, and his hands tensed on her hips.

Always so in tune with his feelings—not necessarily a good thing—she released his neck and smoothed her hands over his chest. "It's okay," she whispered, "we've got this." He nodded, but his hands still dug into the denim of her jeans. "We can take it slow if you want. It doesn't even have to be tonight, if this is weirding you out," she added.

It was weirding him out, but not in the way she thought. Yes, it was incredibly hard to put aside past feelings with Liv in his arms, her face so close to his, her lips—yeah, her lips so wet from her just licking them.

But the thing that was so odd, so weird, was that the body he remembered so well seemed to be on a different woman.

Of course, he'd noticed Liv's changes over the past seven years. When they'd dated and were married, she'd always deferred to him, which had exhausted him, truth be told. She waited for him to initiate sex and let him lead the whole time. Their sex life had always been robust and passionate, even up to the end. But it had always been Twain in the lead.

Liv falling into his arms tonight and soothing away his hesitation? Well, quite frankly, it was a nice change. But it was definitely a change.

One he'd better get on board with fast, or she was going to think he didn't care for the new, slightly aggressive Liv. Let's face it, she might have made the first move, but she was still no man-eater.

And he did care for it. For her taking the lead. Very much.

Which, if her hand dipped a little lower, she'd soon discover for herself.

"It's not weirding me out," he lied to her. A little lie, because whatever trepidation he may be feeling about New Liv was immensely overshadowed by how damn hot the whole thing was to him.

"Good," she said, then pushed on his chest until he fell back to the floor. She slid her legs over his and straddled him, keeping her hands moving along his chest until she got to his shirt buttons, which she started undoing.

She looked down at him, and he slid his hands up her hips to her back and tried to pull her down to him for a kiss.

Other than the small, chaste kiss of thanks she'd given him earlier, it had been seven long years since they'd really kissed. He found he was looking as forward to kissing Liv as he was to having sex.

Okay, almost as much.

She leaned down, and he tried to direct her head to his. But she veered at the last minute and instead kissed his neck, which was now bared of his flannel shirt collar, which she'd unbuttoned and spread open.

Ducking his head, he once more tried to kiss her, but she rose up again and started tugging his Henley from his jeans. She wouldn't meet his eyes, pretending that it took all her concentration to pull a knit shirt free from denim.

Oh. She didn't want to kiss him. That made sense, probably. A way for her to protect her feelings. A way for them both. They could just get on to the main event.

Every guy's dream, right? No foreplay. And yet a sadness seeped through Twain that he tried to hide from Liv.

So it was going to be some kind of *Pretty Woman* twist where no kissing was involved, just a down-and-dirty transaction.

Did that make him the whore?

He was starting to think he'd give the kissing thing one last shot when a phone went off from somewhere close.

"It's not mine," he said, rising to his elbows, hoping she would disregard the ringing. And it looked like she wanted to, her eyes now on the bare skin of his stomach, her finger slowly tracing the line of hair that ran deep into his jeans.

He willed her to keep that finger gliding as the phone continued. He opened his mouth to tell her to silence the damn thing when a thought came to him at apparently the same time as it did to Liv.

"Matty," they said at the same time.

She reached behind her and pulled a phone from the back pocket of her jeans. He'd seen the outline of it earlier when she was studying the wall of skis and he was studying her luscious ass.

"It's not his ringtone, but still…" she said as she pulled the phone in front of her.

"Yeah, of course," he said. He peeked at the clock on Matt's nightstand—midnight.

"Hello? Susan?" Liv said as she connected. She must have Susan Porter's contact info in her phone from when they'd been in Marquette. "Is Matty okay?"

The look on her face had Twain sitting up all the way, hanging on to Liv so she wouldn't topple backward. He leaned closer to hear, Liv holding her phone out a bit to help. "…I don't think it's anything to worry about, but of course, I wanted you to know."

"I'm in Calumet right now, but can be there in twenty minutes."

"Umm…yes, maybe you should come down. Like I said, I'm sure they're fine. But until we find them…"

Find them? He opened his mouth to ask questions—of Liv or Susan—but Liv placed a finger over his mouth, meeting his eyes and giving her head a little shake.

"I'm sure you're right. Just being boys, I guess. I'll be there as fast as I can, Susan. Thanks for calling."

"I'm so sorry, Liv," he heard the woman say. Twain felt sorry for Susan and her husband. To have your kid mess up was one thing, but to have someone else's kid mess up on your watch? Hard.

"It could have happened to any of us, Susan. Don't worry, we can strangle them together," Liv said with a little laugh, which Twain would lay odds on was all for Susan's benefit.

Liv disconnected and started to rise off him. He helped her up and then followed. "They snuck out of the Porters' basement," she said, filling in the blank, though Twain had surmised as much. She was out the bedroom door with him following as he tucked his knit shirt back in and started doing up the buttons on his flannel.

At the bottom of the stairs, she looked around for her coat. "I'll drive," he said, handing it to her and retrieving his from the hook behind the front door.

"You don't need to go," she said. "I'll call when—" She wisely stopped when she saw the expression on his face. "Yes, of course. You'll want to come. But we should drive separately. We can't drive up to the Porters' together in your truck at one a.m."

He shook his head. "You need to be able to text and call. I'll drive. Who cares what they'll think," he said, grabbing his truck keys from the bowl he'd made from a large tree root, which sat on a small table in the foyer. "Might as well get started on the whole town knowing our private business thing now," he said, leading her through the front door.

"I'm willing to put up with that for a baby," she said as he opened his truck door for her, "but not so much for my kid being a teenager testing his boundaries."

He was surprised how calm she was being. He would have guessed she'd be crying or at least much more upset, but she seemed to be taking this all in stride.

"Is that what you think this is? Just two boys testing boundaries?" he asked when he got into the driver's seat. He turned the heat on full blast. Since he hadn't put the truck in the garage when he'd gotten home from work, they had to wait while the defroster did its magic.

"Teenage stuff, yeah," Liv said, her fingers out of her multicolored knitted mittens and tapping on her phone. "It was bound to happen. I guess it starts now."

"You're being really calm about this," he said.

She shrugged. "We raised a good kid with a good head on

his shoulders. We're still going to punish him for this stunt—we can figure out a punishment together—and have one hell of a talk with him about the dangers out there now that you and I never had to worry about."

Twain shuddered at the thought. Literally shuddered. "Christ," he said, putting the truck in gear as the windshield became manageable.

"But ultimately, he's going to have to start taking responsibility for his actions. We gave him the tools, the foundation of right and wrong, safe and dangerous. If he abuses the trust we placed in him, he'll pay the price."

"Wow, you're being so…rational," he said, and she laughed.

"I know, right? I believe all of what I just said, I really do. But a part of me is freaking out, I'm not going to lie."

"A *big* part of me just wants to wring his skinny, little neck," he said.

She smiled at him and moved her hand to place it on his arm, but her phone went off at that moment. She picked up the call.

"Have they shown up yet?" she asked. He couldn't hear Susan from where he sat, but Liv shook her head at him, while Susan kept talking. "Oh. Well, that explains why he hasn't texted or called me back." She listened again, then said, "You know what? Why don't you wait on that until I get there. I'm just leaving my sister's now, and I'm going to swing by Twain's house and let him know. I'm sure he'll want to come with me. Let's wait until then before we start waking up and worrying other parents, okay? Unless you think they might be hurt or something?" She was nodding, in agreement with whatever Susan was saying. "Me too. Okay. Be there soon." She hung up and looked out the side window.

"Let's hope Susan Porter doesn't know your sister."

Liv turned her face to him and smiled. "She doesn't. We're safe. You're right, though. If I get pregnant, the cat will be out of the bag soon enough. I just figured why start it early."

"That's cool," he said, wondering why he felt a little tweaked that Liv was so desperate to keep secret the fact that she was with him.

Rationally, he got it. But this night had been anything but rational.

"What did Susan say?"

"That the boys left their phones in the basement."

"Why?"

She shrugged. "So we couldn't GPS them, I'm guessing."

"Shit, that's a thing? We could be doing that?" The thought was both alarming and comforting to Twain. "*Should* we be doing that?"

"We have the capabilities with our phones, or at least with my phone. But I've never done it. Never felt I needed to…"

"Before."

"Right."

"So, yeah, let's talk about that punishment."

They had Matty's penance figured out and had heard no more from Susan by the time they were at the Portage Lake Lift bridge connecting Hancock to Houghton.

"Where do the Porters live?" he asked.

"By Tech, up Agate. But you know what? Let's try something else first."

"Okay. What?"

"Do you know where Sawyer's partner Andy Summers lives?"

He thought back in his memory. "No. I know it's in Houghton but that's it. Why?"

"Just a suspicion."

"You think Matt and Justin are, what? Over having a late night chat with Andy Summers?"

"He has a daughter Matty's age. Heather."

Twain stayed silent, memories of his son on the ski hill playing through his mind. "Let me guess, she has purple ski boots and poles."

Liv gasped, turning to look at him as he turned right after the bridge taking him to the Houghton waterfront. He pulled his truck into the lot of—crazy coincidence—Summers and Beck engineering.

"You knew he liked her? Did he talk about her with you?"

He shook his head as he put the truck in park and pulled his phone from his coat pocket. "Not a word. But he's always sniffing around her at the hill. I guess I kind of thought she wasn't interested." He called Sawyer on his phone, and after a quick conversation with his drowsy brother, he hung up and handed the phone to Liv.

"Sawyer's going to text me Andy's address and phone," he said, and seconds later, the text tone for Sawyer dinged.

"Up behind ShopKo," Liv said, reading his phone. "Maple Street."

As he headed that way, he said, "Call Andy and give him a heads-up that there may be a party going on in his basement and that we're minutes away." Liv looked at Twain's phone, her hand poised above it. "If you feel pretty confident that's where Matty is," he said.

She sighed, nodded, and began tapping on the phone. "Yeah, I'm almost certain."

"You're sure you want to go through this all again?" he asked, teasing in his voice. "With another kid?"

She took her finger from the phone and looked over at him, a wide smile on her adorable face. "Surprisingly, yes. Definitely yes."

He smiled back at her. "Me too."

Thirteen

—⚬⚬—

LIV RETURNED TO HER OFFICE FROM TAKING MATTY TO the airport, to find a large bouquet of flowers on her desk. *Twain.*

Now that Matty was off to Florida to visit her parents for his spring break, she and Twain would be able to start...*trying* again.

This past week, since the night they'd picked up Matty from the Summers' home, their son had been grounded, so there had never been a good time for Liv and Twain to sneak away.

They'd also taken away Matty's phone for the week, and he was working for Twain after school without pay. And they'd been long hours, as Twain was staying late, trying to get as much done as possible before road restrictions were put in place.

While driving to pick up Matty from the Summers' home, they'd toyed with the idea of cancelling Matty's trip to visit her parents over break. But the plane ticket had long been paid for, and her parents were really looking forward to their youngest grandchild's visit. It would have been a far-reaching penance that would affect more than just Matty, so they'd allowed the trip to stand.

Which, if these flowers were any indication, would also serve as time for them to create the baby she ached for.

It was a sweet gesture. In fact, she couldn't ever remember Twain sending her flowers to work before. When they'd been married, he quite often brought her wildflowers that he'd picked in the woods, which she always put in the beautiful crystal vase

Molly had given her at Liv's bridal shower. But never flowers from a florist sent to her office.

Not that he hadn't been thoughtful, but the majority of the gifts and surprises he'd given her were things he'd made. Which, quite honestly, were much more precious to her than flowers that needed to be thrown away after a few days.

But to get this lovely bouquet today, when Matty had just left for a week, signaled to Liv that Twain was fully on board with her desire to have another child. And to get started on it…now.

"Oh good, you're back," Liv's coworker Cathy said as she came through Liv's door. "I've been dying to know who sent those to you. But by the look on your face, I'm guessing you already know who they're from." She sat on the edge of Liv's desk close to where Liv stood. "You've been holding out on me, Liv," Cathy said with a kidding tone, that Liv knew wasn't all that joking.

Cathy Brandon was Liv's closest work friend, office confidante, and occasional Friday after-work wine (and whine) partner. A few years older than Liv, Cathy bordered on being bitter with life, but had treated Liv well, even when Liv had been promoted to the dean's assistant three years ago, leaving Cathy in the cubicle administrative area. Round and tidy, with short, slightly graying hair, Cathy wore sensible shoes, slacks, and a silky blouse with a large collar under a cardigan nearly every day. The colors changed, and in the summer, the cardigan was placed on the back of her chair and the blouses switched to short-sleeved.

Liv hated holding out on her friend, but there was no way Liv was going to share with Cathy her plan to have a baby with Twain. At least not until Liv could no longer hide a pregnancy.

She wouldn't be sharing her plan with anyone until it was a reality and she was well into her second trimester. Cathy—and others—would no doubt try to talk her out of having a baby with Twain if they knew beforehand. All her friends held Twain responsible for the end of their marriage.

"They're probably from my parents," she said to Cathy. "Trying to cheer me up because Matty will be gone for a week."

Cathy looked at her suspiciously, and Liv knew her friend hadn't bought it. That was confirmed when Cathy nodded at the card stuck to the top of the gorgeous bouquet. "Read it."

Liv knew better than to wait for Cathy to leave before reading the card. Her friend wouldn't go as far as looking over her shoulder, though. Liv pulled the card from the holder and moved behind her desk as she slid it from the envelope, happy to see it was still sealed. As she turned, she told herself to put on her best poker face so that nothing gave away that the flowers were from Twain and not her parents as she'd said.

But her face could not hide the shock of the message she read.

I miss you. Let's talk. Kevin.

"What?" Cathy said, sensing Liv's surprise like a shark smells blood in the water.

"I...I..." Liv just shook her head and handed the card to Cathy. *This* she was happy to share with her somewhat meddlesome friend. Because *this* was a no-brainer.

"Oh my God," Cathy said, putting voice to Liv's thoughts. "What nerve. I can't believe he thought you'd discuss getting back together."

"I know," Liv said quietly, still in shock from Kevin's message. In her mind, there was nothing left unsaid, no closure needed. Liv knew she could not be in a relationship with Kevin just for the sake of having another child. It wasn't even so much the cheating but more realizing how little she cared. That she'd only stuck with the relationship for the chance to have a child. When she'd confirmed her suspicions that he was cheating, she'd cut her losses and walked, telling him in no uncertain terms that it was over.

"As if you'd ever forgive him for cheating on you," Cathy said.

"Lots of people do," Liv said absentmindedly as she sat down at her desk. Cathy placed the card down in front of her, the cream paper almost blending in with the color of her desk blotter. It could have been on flaming-red card stock as out of place as it felt to Liv to have it in front of her.

Honestly, she hadn't thought of Kevin for more than a second or two since they'd broken up three months ago. That in and of itself was telling, seeing as she'd thought of Twain every day in the past seven years.

"Yeah, I suppose," Cathy said, plunking down into one of the two chairs across the desk from Liv. "I mean, if you have kids and stuff, it doesn't necessarily have to be a deal breaker, and I'm sure *some* people work it out." Liv ran her finger across the top of the card while she listened to her friend. "But it seems like you'd always be wondering, right? Like that old 'once a cheater, always a cheater' thing would always be in the back of your head."

"Hmmm," Liv murmured, wondering if Cathy's words were true. Would it always be there? Could you never forget, even after you long ago forgave? Even after seven years?

"Liv? You're not seriously considering meeting with him, are you? You wouldn't get back together with him, right?"

"Kevin?" she asked, like there was another option.

When clearly to Cathy there wasn't. "Yes, of course Kevin."

"No," Liv said. "Not a chance." There was a conviction in her voice that brooked no argument.

"Of course not," Cathy said with a firm nod. Then she looked across the desk at Liv, her head tilting. "Poor Liv. To have been cheated on twice in your life. First with Twain and then with Kevin. It's just not right."

"Twain was…different."

"Of course. That was worse. You were married and had a kid. It's so not fair that you've gone through this twice now."

Liv gave her well-meaning friend a small smile. "No. Well, who said life was fair, right?"

"Ain't that the truth," Cathy, who was divorced herself, said. She hoisted herself out of the chair and nodded toward the bouquet. "Nice flowers, though." As she left Liv's office, she turned to give a "You're sure you're okay?" look to Liv. When Liv nodded, Cathy left to return to her cubicle. They would only be needed in the office today, with the rest of the week being Tech's spring break.

Liv pulled her phone out of her purse to send two very different texts to two very different men.

Thank you for the flowers. Nothing has changed on my end, so no need to meet. Be well.

Matty safely on plane. My place tonight after you're done.

She thought it particularly bold of her to not even end it with a question mark.

Fourteen

—⚋—

WHEN TWAIN PULLED INTO LIV'S DRIVEWAY, HER GARAGE
door was up and her Escape was parked to one side, leaving a
space—he assumed—for his truck next to it.

He pulled into the garage, figuring if he was wrong about his
assumption he could easily move the truck back to the driveway
or even onto the road.

He'd been thrilled when he'd finally read Liv's text hours after
she'd sent it. It'd been the first break he'd taken, and he usually
didn't even check his phone when he broke for lunch or coffee,
the woods being arbitrary when it came to a cell signal.

But knowing Matty was leaving today (they'd had dinner
and said their goodbyes last night), Twain had taken a chance and
checked his phone to make sure his son had gotten away with no
problems.

There was a recent one from Matt sent to both Twain and Liv
stating he'd arrived safely in Fort Meyers and was at his Koskela
grandparents' home.

He responded to his son, but then quickly flicked back to
see that Liv had also sent a text, wanting him to stop over on his
way home. Nothing about wanting to talk, or pick something up,
or about Matt. It was an obvious invitation for baby-making sex.
One to which he responded in the affirmative right away.

"Hi," Liv said from the door leading into the house.

"This okay?" he asked, pointing at where he'd parked his truck. She nodded and pressed the button at the side of the door, closing the garage door as he made his way to her.

"I just thought it might be better. Obviously, the neighbors have seen your truck at my house, but a lot of them know Matty's in Florida. And I—"

He held up a hand. "No worries. I totally get it."

She stood aside as he passed her at the door, but he brushed against her, though he really could have cleared the door without having to.

Dressed in a long sweater she'd probably made, leggings, and wool socks with different-colored toes, she had her long hair up in a ponytail, as she often had when she got home from work when they'd been married.

She looked just like the eighteen-year-old he took home from Paula Ilonen's party all those years ago.

"Cute socks," he said, moving into her kitchen.

She wiggled her toes, a smile on her face. "They are cute, aren't they? They're not quite ready to sell, though. I need to work out a way to get them thinner without the cost of an angora yarn or something that fine."

He knew she sold her knitting as a side business because she had done some craft shows when they'd been married. At the time, they'd really needed any extra money. But watching as Liv balanced a hand on the kitchen table and studied the sock on her foot, Twain realized that she must have branched out beyond selling scarves and mittens at the various craft shows across the Upper Peninsula during the summer months.

"You'll figure it out," he said, and knew his words were true. Before, Liv would ask his opinion on everything, wanting his input, afraid to make a decision on her own. That had obviously changed when they split up.

"I know," she said, proving his point. "And it's been fun making prototypes." She seemed to see him then, taking in his fresh-from-the-woods appearance. Sawdust, dirt, and grime included.

"Sorry," he said. "I swung by Huck's to shower, but there were a bunch of cars in front. Looked like he had people over. And I didn't want to take the time to go all the way to Calumet and back—"

Because he couldn't wait to have sex with his ex-wife? Instead, he'd shown up at her place looking like he'd been fighting with a pine tree all day. And the pine tree had won.

He'd been thinking about putting in some showers at the office. Now that project moved up higher on his list.

"No, of course not. That would be silly to go all the way to Calumet and then back. Why don't you just use my shower?"

He nodded. That was what he'd concluded when he'd driven by Huck's and had seen that his little brother had a full house. But now, the thought of using Liv's shower seemed so...intimate.

Ha. He was about to put himself inside her body, but using her shower was too intimate?

"I can use Matt's," he said, carefully taking off his coat so he wouldn't drop bark or dirt on her kitchen floor.

"No, use mine. You know we designed it with nights like this in mind—you coming home from the cold. Those dual showerheads will be just the thing you need."

They'd made jokes about the shower when they were designing the house with Sawyer, Twain whispering to Liv that he couldn't wait to get her positioned just so under the mid-body showerhead.

But they'd been divorced by the time Liv and Matt had moved in, and Twain had never even seen the finished bathroom, let alone showered in it.

He followed her to her bedroom, and she stepped back, waving him in to the room and the en suite bath beyond. "Towels are in the linen closet. Help yourself to whatever."

"Okay, thanks," he said. "I'll be quick."

"Take your time," Liv said. He watched her bottom sway beneath the cream wool of her sweater as she walked out of the bedroom.

Twain stepped into the bathroom and took two towels from the closet. He grabbed a third and laid that one on the bathroom floor to catch his dirty clothes as he disrobed.

He always kept a clean change of clothes in his truck in case he stayed at the office or at Huck's place if the weather was really bad, but he hadn't wanted to assume that Liv would want him to use her shower, so he'd left them in the truck.

Since the truck was in the garage, he supposed he could just collect his gym bag of clothes wrapped in a towel after his shower.

Or hell, maybe Liv would be waiting in bed for him when he got out, and they'd commence with their homemade fertility treatment.

The thought of Liv warm and naked under her covers made the peeling of his thick pants, long johns, and briefs particularly hard.

Yeah, hard, all right.

It took him a second to get the jets and nozzles where he wanted them for maximum pressure and heat on his aching muscles. In their apartment, Liv would often join him in his evening shower if Matty was already down. But even then, it hadn't really been Liv's idea. Twain would give her shoulder a squeeze as he walked by on his way to the bathroom. One of those marital cues that couples developed over time. Like saying "I'm going to bed…are you coming?" to your spouse, or a hand on the other's hip as you lie awake in bed reading.

For them, it had been the squeezing of Liv's shoulder for shower sex. That shower had been tiny compared to the spacious, walk-in style with tiled bench in which Twain now held his head directly in the stream of hot water.

Remembering the times in the tiny apartment's shower only added to the ache of nostalgia Twain felt.

And also added to his hard-on.

It wouldn't make sense to jack off now, when he needed to be ready to go for Liv. But he'd been on edge since the night that Matt snuck out of the Porters' house. Ever since Liv had launched herself at him in that take-charge way she'd never used when they'd been married. It had totally done it for him, and he'd been semi-hard ever since.

Not that it had ever taken much to be turned on when it came to Liv. Physical attraction had never been an issue with them when they'd been married. And if Twain was honest, it was still a non-issue, as far as he was concerned.

He'd had a few girlfriends in the past seven years. None serious, Twain not even being close to wanting to bring someone into Matt's life. And he'd had even more hookups for a night or two, or a weekend, or whatever.

But whenever he'd seen Liv during Matt hand-offs, he'd always been aware that his physical desire for her had never completely gone away.

And now he was going to have her. One arm leaning against the wall, he reached down with his other hand to stroke himself. Not to get off, but just to ease himself a little bit, his thoughts of Liv taking him to full staff.

Just as he put his hand on his hard cock, he heard the shower door open and felt Liv's small, soft hand on the middle of his back.

"Why don't I do that?" she whispered, and he nearly came right then.

His back still to her, he took his hand from his dick and put it on the shower wall with his other one, raising them both high in a police-frisking stance. One of the nozzles was beating down on his head from the rainfall showerhead. Another stream hit him at his right hip, loosening tight muscles.

Even when she'd join him in the shower in the past (after the shoulder-squeeze cue), he still took the lead as he always did in their sex life. He waited now, baring himself to her—literally and figuratively—to see if she would still need to be led, or if the New Liv from a week ago in Matt's room was still present.

"Have at it," he said.

Fifteen

GOD, HOW SHE'D MISSED TWAIN'S BIG, STRONG BODY.
Leaning her front into his back, she pressed her breasts against
him, eliciting a hiss from him. She knew how he felt; the contact
nearly made her gasp.

She was glad she'd changed her mind about not wanting to
be with Twain at her house. This felt…right somehow, to be here,
in the home they designed together, trying to create a new life.

Resting her cheek on his back, she slid one hand around to
grasp his thick erection. A deep moan came from Twain, and she
tilted her head slightly to be able to kiss his back.

Yes, this was much safer. Shower sex where they were standing
and not lying in bed staring at each other. She didn't trust herself
enough for that.

The night at Twain's place, she hadn't previously consciously
decided to not kiss him. But after she gave him that brief
kiss of gratitude for providing Matty with so much love and
thoughtfulness, she knew she'd never be able to *really* kiss Twain
and not have all her old feelings rekindle. For they would surely
burn her again.

But his body, his back…this she could kiss and nuzzle, and
yes, even lick, without the fear of falling into the chasm of loving
Twain Beck.

To prove her point, she flicked her tongue out and ran it
across his muscles, so toned and taut from his years of chopping,

hauling, and wrangling huge logs.

He tasted of salty sweat, which was quickly washing away to leave no taste at all. Yes, easier. The scent coming from him was so Twain—dirt, the forest, sweat—and conjured up so many memories that she quickly grabbed for her shampoo bottle with her free hand and poured a small glob on his head. Reaching up, she took her other hand away from stroking him, causing a groan, which quickly turned into a moan of pleasure as she massaged the shampoo into his scalp, taking away the unique scent with which he came to her and replacing it with one with no emotional ties.

She had to rise on her toes, and he needed to lean his head back, but she spent a fair amount of time working her fingers through his soft, thick, nearly black hair.

The soapy lather glided down his back, taking small twists against his well-defined muscles, like a stream twining its way past a rocky shore.

She put pressure on his neck to move forward so the rainfall shower aimed for the top of his head and the sluice of waterfall continued to wash away the suds, leaving clear water to rush down his back and over his rock-hard ass. Her hands followed, and she once again reached around, finding him even harder, if that was possible.

"Liv," he said, turning around to face her, twirling them both so her back was up against the smooth tile wall. Lifting her gaze, she almost swallowed her tongue seeing the blatant hunger in his green eyes. He lowered his head, but she moved hers, ostensibly to put her head in the flow from the shower, wetting her hair. One quick glance let her know she hadn't fooled him, but he didn't attempt to kiss her again.

At least not on the mouth.

But oh, that clever mouth of his found other places that had her trembling. Her jaw, an earlobe, her neck. And yes, finally, he made his way to her aching breasts and feasted upon her as if he was as starved as she.

"Twain," she gasped, not able to stop herself. And then she

stopped trying. Yes, she would protect herself as much as possible by not feeling his mouth deeply touching hers. And yes, this act was only for procreation purposes. There would be no tearful reunion with the man she'd loved for years. She didn't want that even if he was offering.

Which he wasn't.

But that didn't mean she couldn't enjoy these glorious sensations running through her body, so hot they tempted to make the steamy water that swirled around her seem like ice.

He bent low, paying attention to one breast, teasing, sucking, tasting, then moving to the next one. Water from the rainfall would hit them haphazardly as his body moved, ricocheting sheets of water onto her torso, splashing into her face.

Twining her hands in his wet and silky hair, her arms lowered when he did, sinking to his knees in front of her. She tried tugging on him. "Twain, you don't need—"

"Shhh," he murmured right before he slid one of her thighs over his broad shoulder and placed his mouth on her.

A few quick flicks with his tongue had her leaning her head back against the shower wall, but she angled so that she could watch his dark head as he brought her to near peak, then backed off. Once. Twice.

Then he looked up at her, no surprise on his face that she was watching him. He spread her even wider, added a finger inside her, and dealt the deadly blow of sucking her in the exact spot that he knew made her implode.

Her legs quivering, she mustered all her strength not to give way. She couldn't hide the physical reactions, but there was no need to let him know how easy it had been for him to get her off.

But the smile in his green eyes and an "It's like riding a bike" grin through his three-day beard had her laughing.

"Show-off," she said, and he just laughed as he kissed his way back up her body, which still trembled from the aftershocks. And also because he had slid another finger deep inside her and kept up a nice, slow, agonizing stroking motion.

Standing, he leaned his back into the water flow, letting it stream down his face, washing her from his lips.

So familiar, so sweet, the memories that played through her mind of this exact motion. He would next bend down and kiss her, letting her taste the lingering essence of her on his water-wet mouth.

Not wanting that to happen (okay, wanting it very badly to happen, but knowing it shouldn't), she pushed at his big chest, propelling him back to the side of the shower, putting pressure on his shoulders to make him sit on the tiled bench that ran the width of the large shower.

Finally, something that they hadn't had in their previous life. A modicum of emotional sanity returned to her. Perhaps they weren't destined to recreate their lovemaking of the past. This new for-baby-only sex could be fun and pleasurable. Orgasms were a bonus she need not be denied.

He looked at the bench for a second, seemingly registering it as a possible tool, and then reached out and wrapped a meaty arm around her waist, pulling her close. Grabbing two washcloths from the in-wall recess, he put one on each side of his hips. Then he lifted her, spreading her legs to straddle his lap, her knees landing on the soft cotton of the quickly saturating washcloths.

The kindness of him thinking of her knees touched her, and she placed a hand softly on his cheek. He turned his head, placing a soft kiss on her palm.

Thinking of her knees was just a small token compared to what he was giving her on this night—a chance at a child she desperately wanted.

God, he was such a good man. Had always been happy to give her what she wanted, what she needed. She'd been too afraid to ask for it. To ask for anything more than what he'd given up to marry her and be a father to Matty.

And even now, the questioning in his eyes as he kept his cheek burrowed into her palm. He would allow more, she knew. He would be open to her showing how much she loved him. He wouldn't hold it against her later. He never had.

But she was a different woman now. Yes, she still loved Twain Beck, but she now also knew her worth. And she was worthy of a man who felt about her the way she felt about him.

As if to prove that she was different, more to herself than to him, she rose from the bench and stepped back away from him. At his raised brow, she tried to paste on a flirty smile as she turned around, her back to him. She looked over her shoulder at him, then took a step closer, sitting down on his lap.

Quick on the uptake as ever, Twain spread his legs, creating a seat for her, wrapping an arm around her waist and urging her up so he could place himself where they both wanted him. Easing down onto him, she leaned forward, spreading her legs so they hung over his thighs, dangling, feet not quite reaching the floor. She balanced her hands on his knees, grabbing on as he came fully into her.

Her body stretched to accommodate him, a feeling of burn easing to fullness. It had been seven years since he'd been inside her, and yet it seemed like both forever and just yesterday.

She didn't have a clear memory of the last time they'd had sex, because of course, at the time, neither of them had ever imagined that it was to be their last time.

"Liv, Christ," he said on a large exhale, his head dropping forward, his mouth finding the tender skin between her neck and shoulder.

As she leaned back against his chest, her hands came up and behind her head, holding on to him as he started to thrust up into her. But it wasn't enough, not nearly enough. She leaned forward again, finding leverage with her hands, scooting them both forward until the balls of her feet found enough purchase on the tile floor so that she could ride him.

And ride him she did.

"Jesus, yes, that… Yes," he said between his thrusts, her movements, and their shared gasps.

Yes, this she could handle. Being one with Twain and yet not having to see those delicious green eyes, the strength of his jaw, the desire she knew he felt. As they gained momentum, the thought excited her. She didn't have to hide anything this way. She could let all the feelings rush over her, and they did, tumultuous and delirious, and she reveled in the sensation that she was once again joined with Twain Beck.

"Twain," she gasped, allowing herself even that—the bliss of yelling his name as she rode him. His hands came forward, one rising to her breast, the other down below, burying in her curls, feeling where their bodies joined.

"Liv, yes," he groaned, his knees rising with his upward movements. When he knew she was near (and she both loved and hated that he could still tell), he both pinched her nipple and slid a finger against her clit. Her body began to spasm around him.

She felt him come, the warmth inside her as good a feeling as his big body draping over her, his arms locking tight around her.

For a baby, she told herself—only for a baby.

She almost believed herself.

Sixteen

—⁓—

"DO YOU WANT ME TO GO?" TWAIN SAID TO LIV AS HE wrapped a towel around himself and—reluctantly—exited the shower. There was no sense staying in once Liv had left him. She sat on her bed, wrapped in a large, pale blue terry bathrobe that nearly swallowed Liv up. Putting the words "swallow" and "Liv" in the same sentence—even mentally—had his body responding again.

She eyed the bulge twitching under his towel. Smiling, she said, "Seems like maybe you should stick around. Double our chances?"

"Maybe even *triple* our chances?" he said, smiling at her.

A slow smile crossed her face. "In that case, I think I need some coffee." She rose from the bed and crossed to the bedroom door. "Want some?" she said over her shoulder to him.

Not especially, but when she smiled at him like that—and was wearing nothing but a robe—he'd pretty much follow her anywhere. "Sure," he said.

He took the time to throw on the clean jeans from his duffel bag that Liv must have retrieved from his truck before she'd joined him in the shower. She would have known one was in the truck; it was a habit he'd had for all his years of logging. So, she must have planned on him staying. At least longer than a quick bang in the shower.

And what a bang it had been.

He still wasn't sure he was cool with the no-kissing business. But the feel of her body moving with his and then against his and the water sluicing down her shoulders onto her back as she rode him had been so damn sexy.

Sex had never been their problem, but there was a give and take in the shower tonight that he wasn't sure he'd experienced with Liv before. An allure to her body, fuller and riper than he'd remembered. More…womanly. And a…confidence, he guessed, in her actions that he found exhilarating. Sexy.

Sure, it had been seven years since he'd touched her as he just had, and people changed. But this time had been different.

He walked down the hallway in nothing but his jeans. The light was off in Matt's room, so he kept on going, although he would have liked to linger in it as Liv had at his place.

A light was on in the room across the hall, and Twain stuck his head in to what was obviously a home office.

But much more than a room with desk, computer, and printer, this was indeed a working office, more like a business workroom and hub.

Whiteboards were on the walls with calendars and shipping tables on them. One wall was all corkboards with "orders in" across the top of one half and—naturally—"orders out" across the other half. Below each column were no less than fifteen sheets of paper, which, upon closer review, were orders for various knitted items.

And it wasn't just for a scarf from a friend. Each order was done with a professional letterhead from *KnitWit,* and the smallest order contained at least five items with a subtotal of nearly four hundred dollars.

Glancing around the room, Twain took in the tables where individual orders were being fulfilled, the rich, bright colors of the items Liv had knitted catching his eye. Under the worktable were flat shipping boxes of various sizes and other mailing paraphernalia.

"Here," Liv said, joining him in the room and handing him a mug of coffee.

"Looks like you've progressed beyond selling mittens during the summer at art fairs," he said, with something that sounded like pride in his voice.

Was he an ass to be proud of Liv? Was it in some way condescending?

She nodded and then took a deep sip from her mug, looking around the room. "About four years ago, things started taking off. Some woman from Chicago happened upon the one cashmere pashmina I'd tried—more as an experiment than anything—at Art on the Rocks in Marquette. She loved it, took my card, and things kind of exploded from word of mouth."

"That's great, Liv," he said. He turned to face her, waiting until her eyes stopped scanning the room and settled on him. He could see the sense of accomplishment in her eyes, and a small ache came upon him that she hadn't been able to find that when they'd been married.

Had he not been supportive? Should he have pushed her more? He'd always told her she had talent, that the things she made were not only fashionable (to his limited knowledge, anyway), but kept him warm even in the outdoors all day. She'd always waved away his compliments.

He made a point now of staring deep into her blue eyes, hoping his sincerity came through in his words. "This totally makes sense, Liv. You always were such a good knitter, made such nice things. It's nice that other people can enjoy them now, too."

He thought for a second she might wave his words away as she'd always done. She even raised her hands as if to make the old motion. But halfway up, her hands stilled, and instead she shoved them in the deep pockets of her comfy-looking robe.

"Thank you. It is kind of great, isn't it?" She smiled, and he had to catch his breath, the sheer joy on her face was so blinding.

"Very great," he said, clearing his throat.

She looked around the room again, a soft flush creeping up her neck and fair cheeks as she realized he was watching her.

He didn't want to embarrass her, but he quite literally couldn't take his eyes off her.

"Well, anyway," she said, walking deeper into the room and setting her mug on her desk, in a mug-shaped clearing of paperwork, mouse pad, and other office supply staples. "I didn't even have a website then. When the Chicago woman bought the pashmina," she clarified for him. He'd been so caught up in what being in this room—basking in her success—did to Liv that he'd lost the thread of her story.

"No website. Right," he said, motioning for her to continue.

"I only had my email on the card I gave her, and that was actually just printed off my computer that morning as almost an afterthought before I went to Marquette."

He knew that many of the weekends he had Matt in the spring and summer that Liv had gone to art fairs throughout the U.P. and Wisconsin. But that was about the extent of his knowledge of Liv and her knitting.

"Thank God, I at least had my email on the card," Liv said. "Anyway, a friend of hers emailed me a few days later saying she wanted one in a different color and asked if she could just order it through my website or via email."

"The website that didn't exist," Twain said, caught up in Liv's excitement of retelling her story.

"Right. Exactly. Well, I dumped all the other stuff I was working on and did nothing but—"

"Cashmere pashminas," he said, though he wasn't even sure he knew what those were.

"Yes! And I found a guy from the IT department at Tech who built websites as a freelancer and got that taken care of."

"And the rest is knitting history," he said with a smile, which she easily returned.

"Kind of, yes. It's been all word of mouth, but it has grown enough that I hired a college student to do order fulfillment and some bookkeeping."

"So that you can knit," he added.

She nodded. "So that I can knit."

He slowly circled the room once more, taking it all in. "Are you able to keep up? This is a *lot* of knitting." He waved to the open orders pinned to the wall. "And looks like it continues to grow."

She nodded. "I've been able to keep up, mainly because I had such a big inventory when I first got noticed. But you're right. I can't handle the potential growth. I'm actually kind of 'auditioning' knitters now."

He smiled. "How do you audition knitters?"

Shrugging, she said, "It's actually pretty easy. I give them the pattern I create, I tell them the color scheme, even supply the yarn, and then see what they come up with."

"Any good candidates?"

She nodded. "Yes, a couple. I want to have a contract written up so that everything is ironclad for taxes and such, and then I'll make offers."

Interested, he asked, "How do you pay a knitter? By the hour?"

"By the piece," she said.

He thought for a moment. How involved did he want to become in Liv's life? In her business? Then he remembered he was here, in her house, just out of her shower, with the intention of becoming even more involved in her life. Having a child together was about as involved as you could get.

"I have some different freelance contracts I've used over the years. Payment by hour or payment by tonnage—which would be like by piece, in your instance. I'll email them to you. It might be a good starting point."

"Oh, okay," she said, surprised. Suddenly he felt like shit. Was it so surprising to her that he'd want to help make her life easier?

"I can set up a meeting with my tax guy for T&B. He's pretty good. He might have some ideas for you."

Again, surprise on her face. "That…that would be great. Thanks, Twain."

He nodded and waved away her thanks as he once again took in KnitWit headquarters.

Matt had never said anything about how Liv's knitting had taken off, but from what Liv had said, Matt would have been around twelve at the time it first began. Twelve-year-old boys didn't pay a keen eye to their mother's knitting business.

If Twain remembered right, Matt's twelve-year-old eye had only been keen on getting to use the smallest chainsaw in *very* supervised situations.

"I'm not getting rich off of it or anything, but…"

"You love it," Twain supplied for her, and she agreed via a small smile.

Early in their marriage, they agreed that Liv would take the administrative job at Tech that she'd been able to secure. It had been low level and not work she enjoyed, but they'd decided that they needed one of them to have a job with good benefits for Matt. Logging would never be that. But Twain had loved it. Still did.

"I'm really glad you found something you love, Liv," he said. She looked startled, and he ran a hand through his drying hair. "Jesus, did I sound like an asshole saying that?"

She shook her head and took a step toward him, but then stopped. "No, you didn't. You sounded happy for me." She took another step toward him, and he stayed very still.

He couldn't take his eyes off her—this woman, so familiar and yet different in many ways. She had definitely changed. The quiet confidence she exuded as she talked about her business, her great accomplishment, was something he hadn't seen on her before.

It suited her. A lot.

She'd brushed her hair when she'd gotten out of the shower, but it was pulled back. Freshly scrubbed, without any makeup, she was startlingly close to the nineteen-year-old he'd married. And yet the evidence in the room they now stood in told the story of a very determined, very talented woman who had turned a hobby she loved into a business.

"Liv," he said, trying to call her to him. She made her way over, and he ran his hands down her arms, linking his hands with hers. She stared up at him, and he knew he had to taste her, had to kiss her.

As if reading his mind, she shook her head, like she was waking from a dream. He held his breath, afraid of what decision she'd come to. Unlacing her fingers from his, she stepped away, and Twain wondered if he would ever taste Liv's mouth again.

Turning to the door, she said over her shoulder, "Was that all talk about doubling our chances, or can you put your…you know…where your mouth is?" She giggled and tore out of the room and down the hall.

A flash of a second and he was behind her, calling out, "You *know* I can put it where my mouth is."

Seventeen

"YOU MIGHT AS WELL SPEND THE NIGHT," LIV SAID LATER. Much later. "What time should I set the alarm?"

Twain moved in the bed beside her. It was amazing he could still move; she herself was nothing more than a lump of languid muscles and some faraway stiffness that threatened to become more pronounced in the morning.

Stiff and lumpy, but glorious. Her well-used body felt absolutely glorious. There was no way she'd be able to get up in—a quick look at the alarm said three a.m.—two hours and be headed for the woods and a full day of physical activity like Twain would have to.

"Umm…just set it for when you have to get up," he said, then flung an arm over his eyes as she turned on the bedside lamp.

Taking the alarm clock in her hand, she said, "I typically get up at seven, and I know you're already on your third cup of coffee by then with the equipment loaded on the trucks."

She looked over at him, realizing she hadn't been privy to his daily habits in seven years. "At least, you used to."

"Still do," he said. "But seven is fine." He peeked out at the clock she held and grimaced, noting the current time and putting his arm over his eyes again. "Yeah, that'll work."

Not needing to set the clock for a different time, she only checked that it was on, placed it back on the table, and turned out the light.

It didn't seem right to burrow into Twain's big body as she had every night when they'd been married. As she very much wanted to now.

It was so odd lying next to him in this bed—one they'd never shared. In some ways, it was so familiar, so…normal. In other ways, mainly when she looked around the room she'd slept in alone for the past seven years, it felt so strange to be here with Twain. Illicit, even. Which, Liv had to admit, was more than a little bit arousing.

She turned, just to be able to see his big, burly body, and he automatically raised his arm for her to come to him.

Which she did with only a millisecond of hesitation.

God, she had always felt so safe in Twain's arms. Afraid and pregnant at nineteen, he had held her and murmured words that allowed her to see a future for them.

When she was a new mother, convinced she was doing everything with Matty all wrong, he would stroke his hand down her arm and reassure her that he was making mistakes too and that they'd figure it out.

They both loved Matty desperately, he'd say, tangling his fingers in her hair as she listened to the steady beat of his heart underneath her cheek. That was the main thing.

When they were both worried about the risk of Twain becoming Eddie's partner, they had lain like they were now and discussed the pros and cons of taking the large step.

Tentatively, she reached her hand out and rested it on Twain's chest, her fingers reveling in the feel of the strong muscles beneath the springy hair.

Kevin had been bare-chested (Liv suspected some manscaping was involved), and she found she much preferred the sheer… manliness of Twain's hairy chest.

Well, of course she did. She preferred Twain to Kevin in every conceivable way.

Twain laid his free hand on top of hers, wiping all thoughts of Kevin Schmidt from her mind. Hard to believe he'd even have the audacity to show up in her thoughts when she was in bed with Twain Beck!

"Hey," he whispered, checking to see if she was still coherent.

"Hmmm?"

"We're really doing this, eh? A baby?"

She smiled, though he couldn't see her face. "Well, if we're not, then we've just had unprotected sex—three times—for no reason."

He playfully pinched her upper arm. "No reason? I think I was just insulted, but I'm too zonked to care."

She giggled, a sound she hadn't heard from herself in a long time. She found she'd missed it. "Yes," she said, answering his original question, "we're really doing this."

"When will we know? If it...worked?"

Liv tried to relax her body, to not tense up at the thought of a one-and-done situation of having Twain's beautiful body at her Beck and call. Not to mention having him inside her, filling her up, making her feel whole again for the first time in seven years.

"I mean, not that we shouldn't keep trying. Doesn't seem... efficient to just try once, wait until we know, and then start over, right?"

"Right," she quickly agreed. "The better the chance and all that."

"Right."

"I've read on some of the pregnancy after thirty-five online sites that some women have tested positive after two weeks."

"Wow, that's fast," he said, with what Liv thought sounded like disappointment in his voice.

She knew how he felt.

"Three weeks seemed to be more of the norm, though. Even that is considered early." His body relaxed a little under her. But there was still the knowledge that this—delightful as it was—was a short-term arrangement for a very specific purpose.

It was with that thought that she said, "You know, I'm off the rest of this week. It's one of the few times that Tech's and

Houghton's breaks lined up."

"Really? Why didn't you go to Florida with Matt?"

She shrugged, and his fingers lightly traced her shoulder. "I was going to spend this week getting a jump-start on designing and patterning items for this fall. And I wanted to let my parents have Matt to themselves, because they so seldom get to see him."

He was quiet, and Liv knew he was reading her—he always could.

"And maybe because you didn't want to have the discussion with your parents about you having another child yet?"

"Maybe," she admitted.

"But you booked Matt's flight months ago."

"Yes." She shifted in his arms, but he held her hand to his chest, sliding his fingers over hers, lacing them together.

"You've been planning on this baby a while, haven't you, Liv?"

"I told you that in Marquette, when I asked you to be the father."

"But you were dating Kevin back when you would have booked Matt's ticket, right?"

"Yes."

"Were you planning on getting pregnant? The two of you? Before you broke up?"

"We'd talked about it, very broadly. He...he..."

"So, all that talk in Marquette about wanting this baby to have the same father as Matt? Was that just part of the sell? Am I the fallback because shit hit the fan with Kevin?" There was no anger in his voice, only understanding. Twain had always understood her.

But this time, he had it wrong.

"No, Twain," she said, rising up to meet his eye. "You were never the second choice. I think that Kevin and I not working out was just what I needed to move forward. Something was holding me back from having a baby with him, and I think it's because this"—she motioned with her hand between them—"was supposed to happen."

"Yeah?" he said, a little skepticism on his face, but also a little hope in his voice.

"Yes. Because, Twain Beck, you were always my first choice."

She started to lie back down, but his hand on her arm stopped her.

"Turn the alarm off. Let's wake up when we want," he said.

She did, and then returned to the warm cocoon of Twain's arms.

Eighteen

—⚏—

IN THE MORNING, THEY DOUBLED DOWN ON THEIR pregnancy chances and then had a big breakfast that Liv made for them both.

"I can't believe you're in road restrictions the same week I have off and Matt's in Florida," Liv said as they sat across the table and drank their second cups of coffee. She was bundled up in that bathrobe again—the one Twain had eagerly peeled off her curvy body last night—her hair done up in a bun at the top of her head. She looked more delicious than the pannukakku that she'd just served him.

"And I haven't done all the testing and stuff yet, and I can be irregular, but this week should be right around when I'm ovulating."

"Yeah?"

She nodded. "Like I said, it's not for sure. I'll buy one of those ovulation indicator things, but I think it's right around now."

"Yeah, that's quite a coincidence, all of that happening in the same week," he said, not really paying attention. His thoughts were on how soon he'd be able to take Liv to bed again. He probably should be paying more attention to the cycle and ovulation talk, but quite honestly, he'd take her at any time, optimum for pregnancy or not.

"It's more than a coincidence. It's a sign, I think," she said, a soft glow surrounding her face.

"Yeah," he said, smiling at her. "A sign? Think that might be a bit much?"

She quickly shook her head. "No, no, I don't. You see, when I was with Kevin, I kept waiting for…"

"A sign?" Twain led for her, his brow quirked up.

She tossed a wadded-up napkin good-naturedly in his direction. "Yes, a sign. Something to let me know that I was meant to have a baby with him."

"Meant to have a baby at all?"

She sat back in her chair, her face turning even…glowier, if that were possible. "No. I *knew* I was meant to have more children. I just wasn't seeing how or when for all those years. But I never doubted that I'd be a mother again."

Suddenly the pannukakku felt like a boulder in his stomach. A rich, delicious, custard-pancake-filled boulder. "So when you met Kevin and started dating, you thought *that* was a sign?"

She looked out the window beside her, taking a deep drink of coffee and holding her mug in both hands. She used to do that in the mornings; have these deep thoughts while looking out the window, cup in hand. Twain could barely think of his own name in the mornings. It wasn't until he was out in the woods, experiencing the bracing fresh air, with the sound of the rustling trees his mental wake-up call, that Twain was able to completely function.

"No. I don't think I thought meeting Kevin was a sign," she said in a way that seemed like maybe she was just figuring that out this very moment. "It felt—and this is unkind, I know—more like a means to an end."

A thousand thoughts ran through Twain's mind, but at the top was one he blurted out before he could stop himself. "Did you love him?"

Slowly—so freakin' slowly—she looked back from the window. Placing her mug on the table, she met his eyes. He tried to keep his face passive, to not let the desperateness he unaccountably felt show on his face.

"No, I didn't love Kevin, though for a while we had a really nice relationship."

Relief flooded through Twain, quickly replaced by shame. If he were the bigger man, he would have hoped Liv would find love, to be happy.

But the asshole in him (the Beck side, no doubt) was gratified beyond belief that she hadn't found it with Kevin Schmidt.

"I have only ever loved you, Twain," she said, still gazing at him with those all-knowing blue eyes.

Ass. He was a total ass, because it took every ounce of energy he had (and after last night—and this morning—he didn't have a ton of it left) to hide the smirk of satisfaction he had at her answer.

"Don't gloat," she teased, rising from the table and taking her cup, and his, to the pot for a refill. "It's unbecoming."

Yeah, yeah it was. But damn if he could hide the smile that burst through.

TWAIN WENT TO THE OFFICE at T&B later that morning to do some paperwork and other things that could be done while they were out of the forests. He had his mechanic in to do general maintenance of the large equipment. The entire time, he was wondering how soon he could get back to Liv.

She had the girl—Chelsea, Liv had called her—who worked for KnitWit coming into her home office from noon until five, so Twain was banished until then.

There was plenty in the office to keep him busy, including following up with bids T&B Logging had out with landowners. But his mind wandered to the night before and memories of entwined limbs, Liv's gasps, and his own hard releases had him closing up shop early and heading into Houghton.

Too early to show up at Liv's, he stopped at the Commodore and had a beer while he waited. He texted her that he'd bring a pizza for dinner, and she responded her approval and confirmation that Chelsea would be there until five.

Part of him bristled at the knowledge that Liv didn't want

him showing up at her house while someone was there. Especially with Matt—and his excuse for being there—in Florida.

And he got it, he really did. Beyond Sawyer, he had no intention of talking about his and Liv's…arrangement with anyone.

Arrangement. What a word for what they were doing. Too civilized to encompass the myriad of emotions that played with him when Liv had slept with her head on his chest as she had last night.

As she had every night.

And much too cold a word to pertain to the scorching desire and arousal he felt just by looking at her body—in the bathrobe or out.

She'd admitted this morning that she'd never loved anyone but him, but she sure seemed more capable than he of keeping what they'd spent so many hours last night—and this morning—doing to an "arrangement" level.

He had an uneasy suspicion that perhaps he was in over his head.

Nineteen

—*m*—

"SO, THE NON-KISSING THING," TWAIN SAID, TAKING A
bite of the cold pizza, which Liv had just brought in from the
kitchen table and placed in the middle of the bed.

He was tangled in the sheets and looked like a very satisfied
Greek god. Was there a god of the woods? She'd have to Google it.
Or a wood nymph? Though there was nothing nymph-like about
Twain's strong body.

She'd thought about heating the pizza up but had wanted to
return to the bed, and Twain, as quickly as possible, so she had
just grabbed the box, napkins, and a couple of beers from the
fridge and returned to her man.

Her man for at least a week.

"Yeah?" she said, crossing her legs, covering a little, but not
a lot, with her robe. She took a bite of the pizza, loving the spicy
sausage that the Commodore used. Even cold, it was good.

And honestly, Twain entering her home, tossing the box of
pizza on the table, and throwing her over his shoulder on his way
to the bedroom was worth eating it two hours later, congealed
cheese or no.

Definitely worth it.

"It feels a little *Pretty Woman* to me."

"So, I'm a hooker, is that it?"

He laughed. "Ha! You're about as much a hooker as I am a

slick corporate tycoon."

She tried to picture him in the sharp suits Richard Gere had worn so effortlessly, but couldn't. Not Twain, no way. But then, there was no way Richard Gere, even back then, could have filled out a plaid flannel shirt like Twain.

"It's not like we've never kissed before, you know," he said.

Oh, she knew. That was the problem. She'd been lost in Twain's Beck kisses from that first night, gladly giving him her virginity because she didn't ever want it to end. "I know," she said, playing with her crust, taking tiny pieces off and placing them in her mouth.

"I mean, a *lot*. We kissed a lot."

She tossed a piece of sausage at him, not even caring that it bounced off his broad shoulder and landed on her lavender sheets, surely causing a grease stain. "I *know*."

He picked the piece of sausage from the bed and popped it into his mouth. "So? What's the big deal? Why won't you kiss me?"

He was being playful, and she intended to be the same way, but when she looked at him, at those teasing green eyes, she spoke with her heart, not with her head.

"Because I have to protect myself, and that's the only way I know how."

He didn't say anything, just looked at her. After an excruciatingly long time, he only nodded.

No "You don't have to protect yourself from me, Liv." No "But we can still kiss." He got it. He knew that she'd been destroyed once and didn't want it to happen again. And because he was at heart a very good man, he didn't want to be the one to destroy her.

Again.

That night, when they had sex, he didn't even try to kiss her. But when they fell asleep, she again lying on his chest, his arm encircling her, pulling her close, he placed the softest kiss on the top of her head. So soft, she thought she might have imagined it. Though she knew she hadn't.

Twenty

—◠◠—

"CAN'T SLEEP?" TWAIN ASKED, AS HE WALKED INTO THE living room, startling Liv.

"No," she said.

"Me neither." He pointed to the television. "Didn't we see this? Like, at the theater?"

She looked up from her knitting to the television that she had on more for background noise than because she was actually watching. *The Notebook* was playing, and she nodded at Twain. "Yes, when it came out. My mom sat with Matt. I asked her because I wanted to see it so badly."

He nodded, scratching his bare chest. He had on his flannel shirt, unbuttoned, and his jeans, also unbuttoned and settling on his hips.

Yeah, better than Ryan Gosling for sure. And that was saying a lot.

She was sitting in the rocker that she chose when she couldn't sleep and was knitting instead. Twain spread his tall body across the couch, his feet hanging over the side.

"But they're the flashbacks, right? There's an older— Yeah, right," Twain said, and Liv saw that the scene had changed to the modern-day setting.

She'd seen the movie many times since that date night with Twain all those years ago, but she was guessing he probably hadn't.

"What's that actress's name?" he asked.

"Gena Rowlands?"

"The young one?"

"Rachel McAdams?"

"Right, right," he said. He pulled one of her knit throws from the back of the couch, threw it over himself, punched a pillow into the correct shape for his head, and then moved his body until he was in optimum viewing mode. "What else have we seen her in?"

"*Mean Girls?*" she said, not looking up from her needles. "*Wedding Crashers?*"

"Yeah, right," he said, burrowing deeper into her couch. "What else?"

"*The Time Traveler's Wife? Sherlock Holmes?*"

"Didn't see those," he sleepily said.

Although the scene of him drowsing on the couch and her knitting with the television on in the background seemed so familiar, the fact that Twain hadn't seen *Sherlock Holmes*, or many other movies, reminded Liv that they had lived separate lives for the past seven years.

And they would see any Rachel McAdams movies separately in the future. She had to remind herself that no matter how easy, how routine Twain's and her actions were this week, it would only be this way until she conceived.

Then it was back to divorce as normal.

And really, it wasn't even until she conceived, but only this week while Matty was gone, that they'd be able to… The phrase that came to mind—play house—made her unaccountably sad.

There had been no playing in her life with Twain. They *had* made a home together, a family. They did have a rich past, full of memories of lovely, mundane things, such as having her mother watch Matt for a rare date night and falling asleep in each other's arms on the couch during a late movie.

Her emotional self-preservation low due to the haze of memories, Liv got up from her chair, placing the blanket she was working on carefully on the table next to the rocker. Quietly, she made her way over to the couch. Apparently she was not quiet enough, because Twain, eyes only open to slits, had his arm up, holding the blanket open for her to join him.

Sliding in, keeping her back to his front, she breathed in deeply as he brought his arm around her, securing the blanket under her chin and then tucking his big hand under her arm. The scent of pine from his shirt—and probably his skin— overwhelmed her, and she took another deep breath, causing her chest to bump into his forearm.

"Liv," he whispered, nuzzling the back of her neck, pushing her hair aside with his chin.

She had only intended to lie with him, to bask in the memories of simpler times. But she could never be this close to Twain and not become affected. And from the burgeoning erection bumping against her back, it seemed that Twain now had other things on his mind than Rachel McAdams' bio.

"God, you smell good," he said, his nose at the nape of her neck.

"I was just thinking the same thing," she said, more to herself.

"Seeing as we've been showering together for two days, we probably smell the same," he said, chuckling.

She shook her head. No. No one ever smelled like Twain to her. It wasn't the shampoo and soap from her shower. It was the outdoors, the trees, the earth. That was the very essence of Twain Beck. "Pine," she inadequately summed up for him.

"Yeah, I can never get the smell of the trees off me, no matter how hard I try."

She put her hand on top of his and led his hand to her breasts. "Don't try," she said.

DAMN, HE LOVED THAT she crawled onto the couch with him. They'd lain this way all the time years ago, but always because he'd beckoned her over or had joined her.

Once again, she had made the first move, and he liked it as much as he had the first time. Maybe even more.

An easy slide and his hand was beneath the lapels of her robe and then in between her soft, ripe breasts.

Her breath rose, and he wound his hand around her top breast, cupping it and then giving a firm squeeze, eliciting a soft moan.

They'd gone at it like rabbits for the past two days, and yet Twain couldn't get enough of her.

Maybe it was knowing they were on the clock, but something was different in the way he thought about Liv. Which was to say, he thought about her all the time. And with a...frenzy that surprised him.

Yeah, it had been a while since he'd been with a woman, and even longer since he'd been with anyone on a semi-regular basis. But this appetite he had for Liv surprised him.

And scared the crap out of him.

The scariness of his feelings was not something he was willing to examine right now. Not with Liv wiggling her bottom against his aching dick.

He flicked his thumb over her hardening nipple. "Twain," she gasped as she pushed back against him again, and he knew it was going to be hard and fast this time. Which was okay with him.

Reluctantly taking his hand away from her breasts—and getting a groan from her—he quickly hiked up her robe in the back, happy to find she hadn't bothered to put on any panties when she'd left the bed.

Pushing the offending terrycloth out of his way, he reached around, and Liv quickly opened her thighs for him, her foot coming up onto his shin to give him room.

Happy to find her wet and obviously as ready as he, he stroked her a few times to get her to where he knew she'd only need a few thrusts once he was inside her. A place he was bursting to be.

Sliding his hand away from her again, murmuring it was okay when she protested, he pulled himself out of his jeans and then pulled her thigh up, over, and slightly behind his.

He pushed back into the soft couch to give himself enough room to reach down to guide himself to her. Instinctively, she leaned back just as he pushed forward, and he slid into her wet heat.

The room was dark but for the changing light of the movie, though Twain wasn't watching the screen. He was propped up on one elbow, watching Liv's face—what he could see of it from his angle—as he began to slowly move inside her.

Her face glowed from more than the ambient light. Eyes closed, her teeth on her lower lip, a tiny bite with each stroke from him. He knew the moment she became aware he was watching her; even without opening her eyes, her demeanor changed.

"No, no," he whispered, lowering his head to kiss her ear as he added, "Beautiful, Liv. Feel it." But it was too late. Her guard, as invisible as she probably thought it was to him, was fully back in place.

She still moved with him, still clenched her muscles tight around him on his downstroke, but the feel, the…rawness to it was over.

He should have been happy. He didn't want to hurt Liv, didn't want her to resurrect feelings that she'd come to terms with long ago.

Did he?

Before he could think on it any longer, the little hitch in her breath that signaled she was close came, and he started moving faster. Seconds later, it was over. She had come. He had come. They were closer to achieving their goal of possibly creating a child.

And yet…

He allowed his attention to wander, and it fell on the television. Rachel McAdams was locked in the hero's arms, rain pouring down around them, music swelling.

Pushing his still-hard cock deeper into her, and getting a gratifying aftershock of muscle tightening from her, he said, "Shit, they got nothing on us."

She laughed, but the sound was halfhearted, unbelieving, which made Twain feel inexplicably sad.

Twenty-One

LIV CAME HOME FROM GROCERY SHOPPING SATURDAY morning to find Twain in Matty's room. Sitting on the bed, he had a framed photo in his hands, a finger tracing along the edge. Without even looking, Liv knew it was a photo taken of the three of them when Matty had just finished with his first ski lesson. They were at the bottom of Mont Ripley, a tiny Matty in between Twain's legs, little skis awkwardly crossed at the tips. Liv standing next to her boys, her face looking up at Twain, her hand on Matty's knit-cap-covered head.

The scene was very familiar to her because oftentimes, when her son was with his father, she found herself exactly as Twain was now—sitting on Matty's made bed, staring at that photo.

"Now I get how you felt that night in his room at my house," Twain said, not looking up from the photo, not even acknowledging her, really.

"How's that?" she asked. She knew, but she wondered if Twain could articulate it better than she had.

He looked up at her and then stood, putting the picture back on the top shelf of Matty's bookcase. "Like the person you love most in the world, the person you think you know absolutely everything about…" He ran his hands over Matty's books on the top shelf, his fingers bumping over the spine edges of the *Magic Tree House* books. Twain had read those books to a young Matty almost every night when he got home from work. Horribly long days that turned into nights, but he made it home in time to read a chapter or two from a *Tree House* book to Matty, sometimes even before he'd taken a shower or eaten something. "And there's a part of him you have nothing to do with," Twain continued, his hand now moving down a shelf to the more easily reached items of graphic novels and the *Game of Thrones* books that Matty was now reading.

Yes, that's exactly what it was like, Liv thought.

"Like there's a double life there. As if he's at some party to which you're not invited."

"Yes, exactly," she said, stepping deeper into the room and sitting in the spot on the bed Twain had just vacated.

"And it's good," he said, twirling around to face her, a pewter figurine of a skier filched from the shelf lying in his hand. "It's good, right? That he has this...this other life."

"Yes, it's good. He's becoming his own person. He's right on track. Starting to pull away and yet still needing us."

Twain nodded, and Liv noticed that his hair was a bit longer than he typically wore it, catching a bit on the collar of his shirt rather than lying right at the edge. She stopped herself from suggesting it was time for a haircut.

That was what a wife would say.

Besides, she kind of liked it longer.

"Right," he said, again nodding. "On track. And it's because he's a teenager, and he's supposed to be pulling away, testing boundaries." There was question in his voice, and Liv nodded. "Not...not because of the divorce."

She quickly rose from the bed and placed a hand on top of his. The skier figurine poked her palm, but she ignored it.

"No. It's not from us both raising him. Separately. Stuff is not falling through the cracks, Twain." He looked down at her, his green eyes searching, as if he were taking great consolation from her words. She squeezed his hand. "He's a teenager finding his way. We're here to make sure he doesn't get off track, but..."

She didn't need to finish. Whatever skittishness being in

Matty's room (and seeing the unfamiliar amongst the known) had brought up in him vanished and the quiet confidence returned to his face.

"And we're going to be okay with the next one, right?"

"That's right," she said. "As long as you're still on board," she added, not knowing why. It might be too late anyway if her hopes came true and she was already pregnant, but something deep inside her wanted to give Twain one last out.

If he wanted it.

She knew some people in town thought she'd gotten pregnant on purpose to keep Twain when he'd gone to Tech. She knew she hadn't, and she believed he didn't think it, but she didn't want any doubts about this baby.

"I want it. I want *her*," he said, and the pole of the skier figurine nearly broke her skin, she squeezed his hand so tightly.

"Thank you, Twain," she said, releasing his hand and walking to the hallway. She looked back at the doorway. "I just got some good lunchmeat. How about a sandwich? Are you hungry?"

There was no flirtation in her voice, no innuendo at all, but the grin he gave her had heat flooding through her.

"Starving," he said, and followed her into the hallway.

He took her hand and led her, not to the kitchen but to the bedroom.

THEY HADN'T HAD THAT MUCH sex in a week even when they'd first been married, Twain thought on Sunday morning.

Their last morning together.

They'd changed the sheets several times throughout the week. The current ones were light blue, but they all smelled of crisp, light, flowery detergent. And Liv.

And them.

He heard Liv in the shower and contemplated joining her, but was content to just lie in bed and listen to her hum the theme song from the movie they'd watched on television last night.

Of course, they'd had more sex this week than before, he

mused. When they'd been first married, and finally had a place to themselves other than her car or his dorm room, Liv had had terrible morning sickness and then was huge. Not that they hadn't figured out ways around her growing bump, but they were both always tired.

But not nearly as tired as they would be after Matt was born. And from then on, there was always a baby/toddler/adolescent underfoot, and all-day fuck-fests were out of the question.

But yesterday—Saturday—Twain didn't have to check in at the office and Liv didn't have Chelsea coming for a few hours. Well, they had put a childfree home to good use.

But they still hadn't done it face to face. Though he knew he shouldn't care (fantastic sex was nothing to scoff at), Twain found that it bothered him.

Standing back to front, reverse cowgirl, on the couch back to front, doggy, doggy standing, spooning. It had all been amazing and much more inventive than they'd been during their marriage. And yet it wasn't enough for Twain. Greedy bastard that he was, he wanted to see the blue of Liv's eyes as she came. Wanted to see her mouth as she moaned and called his name.

Wanted to kiss her. Deeply. Passionately. Fiercely.

He knew he could do it, get Liv to kiss him. It wouldn't take much, as their bodies naturally gravitated toward it each time. It was almost an effort to not fuse their mouths together. In that way, the non-facing sexual positions were helpful.

And sexy as shit, to be sure.

But still…

He rose from the bed, not as content to just bask in their shared, rumpled bed as he had been a moment ago. He made his way to the shower and cleared his throat at the doorway so as not to startle her. When he opened the door, she was facing him, clutching a soapy loofah. Her long hair, two shades darker when wet, was slicked back from her face and falling down her back.

"Room for me?" he asked. She smiled and nodded, taking a step deeper into the shower to give him room, but still—

thankfully—facing him.

His gaze raked down her body. Her curvy and full breasts, so different from the girl of nineteen she'd been and yet no less beautiful. More so, in fact.

The soft swell of her tummy, possibly soon to be ripe with his child. Pale, creamy hips and thighs and the secret garden hidden within.

"Beautiful," he whispered, his gaze coming up to meet hers.

Her breath hitched and then started coming faster, as did his own. He told himself not to do it, but couldn't help dropping his eyes to her mouth. To that full, juicy mouth, lips wet either from the shower or just her. Her tongue darted out, licking them, and Twain took a step closer to her.

Her white teeth chewed on her full lower lip, and Twain held his breath, feeling a decision was being made.

He watched as she swallowed, her throat moving. Another tiny step closer to her, he leaned down slowly. So, so slowly.

"Liv," he whispered, tantalizingly close to his prize.

Suddenly, he felt the scratchy mesh of her loofah pushed into his stomach, only inches above his raging hard-on.

"Do my back?" she said, handing him the damn loofah and turning toward the wall.

He did her back. And much, much more.

But he didn't kiss her.

Twenty-Two

"DELAYED BY AN HOUR," LIV SAID, CLIMBING INTO Twain's truck outside the tiny Houghton County airport. "I should have checked from home. I don't know what I was thinking. I should know better with the weather delays we get."

Twain looked out at the bright, clear end-of-March sky. "Really? Looks fine here."

"Apparently they had to de-ice in Chicago."

"Hmm," Twain said. Liv knew that he was thinking that if it was icy in Chicago then perhaps the bad weather would be headed this way and the road restrictions would be lifted.

It was Sunday afternoon. Matt was on his way back, and Twain would soon be back to fourteen-hour days.

It seemed that this…whatever this past week had been…was over.

The airport was just about halfway between Houghton and Calumet, and it didn't make sense to them to make the fifteen-minute trip back to Liv's only to do it again in a half-hour.

"Let's go kill an hour," Twain said, and pulled out of the pick-up area. As he was driving the long road back out to the highway, Twain pointed to a spot off one of the side roads. "That's where Petey Ryan's driving range is going," he commented.

To Liv, it looked like a large field with some large poles with orange plastic tied to the tops spread out across the land.

"They've got a ways to go," she said. The snow had melted a lot since Matty had been gone, a fact she was only noticing now.

Because she'd been in a mind-blowing sex fog for the past week.

At the highway, Twain turned right and headed for Calumet. Liv snuggled into the warm seat and thought about all the other things that had probably happened out in the world during the past week.

She'd spoken to Matty, of course, and he'd texted daily, keeping her up to date on his excursions. She'd called her mom too, to make sure Matty hadn't been too much for her parents. From both parties, it sounded like the week had gone well.

As had Liv's.

Her body was still relaxed and liquid from having sex with Twain this morning, but as the time to pick up her son, and the time that this wonderful bubble would surely burst, drew closer, the warm feeling cooled, and the reality of their situation reared its ugly head.

There would be no more lazy days and nights of taking their time with each other's bodies. If she and Twain were to continue with a pregnancy bid, it would be in hurried, sheltered moments.

Unless she was already pregnant. The joy bubbled up inside of her at the thought.

Then they'd never need to have sex again. And just as quickly, the bubbling joy simmered back down.

"How about it?" Twain said, and Liv realized they were idling in front of Tootie's, a Calumet bar.

"Together? In broad daylight?"

"Is your concern being seen together or being seen drinking on a Sunday afternoon?"

He was grinning at her, and she couldn't help laughing as she answered, "Both, I guess."

"Aww, screw 'em," he said, pulling in a few spots down and killing the engine on the truck. "Come on, we'll have a toast. Your last sip of alcohol, hopefully." He was smiling to himself as he said it, getting out of his side of the vehicle.

"Looks like Deni's car," he said as they passed a Subaru.

Though Liv had ridden in that car when they'd all gone to dinner together in Marquette, she'd been in such a daze that night she hadn't really registered much about it.

All her thoughts had been on asking Twain to father her child.

And now, maybe he had.

She stopped dead on the sidewalk and pulled his arm to stop him, too, which he did with a concerned look on his face. "Are you all right? We don't have to go—" He stopped when she shook her head.

"No. I mean yes, let's go in. But while we're alone, I just…" She looked down and kicked a large clump of snow into the pile of melting mush in the street's gutter. Raising her head, she studied his strong face, the face she'd loved for so many years. "I just want to thank you, Twain. For this past week."

He smiled, but it was small and private, not the big grin he'd had earlier. "It was quite a week. I should be thanking you."

"For the baby," she clarified. "Or at least the chance—"

He placed a hand on her mouth, his fingers bare, his gloves left in the truck. She'd kissed every inch of his body in the past week. Everywhere but his face and mouth. To have his finger on her mouth made her desperately want to reach up and finally kiss his lips.

"I know," he said, and it seemed to encompass so much. Gently removing his finger, he added, "But like I said, I think I'm the one who should be saying thank you." At her confusion, he went on, "Thank you, Liv Beck, for making me realize how much I…*needed* something I never even knew I wanted."

The statement seemed loaded, or perhaps she just wanted to read more into it than he'd meant. "The baby?"

He opened his mouth to speak, but didn't. He looked down

at her, and again she had to will her hands to her sides so as not to reach for him.

"Yeah, the baby," he whispered. He walked the remaining steps to the door of Tootie's and opened it for her.

"Liv! Twain!" came a call from the far end of the long, narrow room as they entered.

"Twain thought that was your car out front," Liv said to Deni as she neared her. There were a few old-timers at the bar that Twain stopped and said hello to, but Liv made a beeline for Deni and Sawyer, sitting side by side on stools that had been pushed very close together.

"What'll you have?" Sawyer said, like it was a common occurrence for Liv and Twain to join him and his girlfriend for a Sunday afternoon toddy in their local bar.

"Umm…" She wondered if she'd give herself away if she just ordered water, and then saw Deni had what looked like a pop in front of her. "What are you having?"

"Diet Coke," Deni said. Liv nodded, and Sawyer got the female bartender's attention—a woman she vaguely recognized as having graduated from Calumet a few years before she had—and ordered a Diet Coke and a bottle of Bud for Twain. He then got up and moved a couple of stools around so that it created more of a square than four stools in a line. He patted one of the seats for her and then handed her the Diet Coke when it arrived.

Twain was just joining them and grabbed his own bottle from the bar, tipping it in Sawyer's direction as a thank you.

"What've you two been up to?" Twain asked his brother. "Up at the Ice Cube?" To Liv he added, "That's what I call Sawyer's place up past the Harbor."

They both nodded, a blush on Deni's face, and Liv imagined the couple had spent the weekend doing…well, exactly what she and Twain had been doing.

Twain and Sawyer launched into talk about Twain's business, and Deni leaned forward and touched Liv on the knee. "I just realized the other day that you're KnitWit."

"Umm…yeah. You mean the knitwear, right?"

Deni laughed. "Yeah, exactly. I love your stuff." To prove her point, she rustled under the parka that was on a stool behind her and pulled out a scarf and mitten set that Liv had made once upon a time. "I bought these, I don't know, six or seven years ago at Art on the Rocks."

Liv nodded. Through the years, she'd seen her stuff on various people at various locations across the Upper Peninsula. It never ceased to give her a small thrill that something she'd created was valued by others.

"You probably bought them from me," she told Deni. "I was doing most of the art fairs by myself back then."

"Huh. Weird, hey?"

Liv took a sip of her pop and sat back against the wooden bar stool. "Very weird."

Deni smiled, a bright, unaffected, charming sight, and Liv immediately got how this woman was able to pull Sawyer out of his ten-year funk.

"So," Deni said, and Liv knew she was going to ask what Liv and Twain were doing in a bar together on a Sunday afternoon. Her body tensing, Liv relaxed when Deni only said, "When Sawyer told me you were the one who'd made my mittens, I found your site online. Who knew you made so many great items. I ordered a pashmina for my mother."

Liv was slightly horrified. "Oh, you didn't have to do that. I would have just given you one. What color would you like?"

Deni waved her away. "No way. Business is business. Even if it is all in the family." She looked around the odd circle the four of them created and then met Liv's skeptical look with a mischievous glint in her eyes. "Well, kind of all in the family, right?"

"I guess," Liv hesitantly agreed. "But really, if you ever want any—"

"I'll go to your website and order it, like I did last week."

Smiling, Liv let it go and took another drink of her Diet Coke.

"All good here?" Twain checked in a few minutes later while Deni was explaining something about wind power being so important to the driving range project for Petey Ryan.

Liv nodded, and Deni wound up her explanation as Sawyer put his arm around her and placed a hand deep in the woman's chestnut hair.

Twain, out of habit, it seemed to Liv, put a foot on the rung of her stool and stood next to her, his hand draping across the back.

No big deal. Two couples having drinks and chatting. She and Twain had had drinks with Sawyer and Molly a couple of times, but it had been hard with Matty. And then Molly got to a point where she couldn't stand being in a place with so many people.

Even the five or six regulars at a place like Tootie's had been too much for her.

Liv watched Sawyer watch Deni as she told Twain that she'd done some sketches for the bar area of the driving range. It was obvious that Sawyer was in deep, and if the look of complete ease on his face was any indication, the hermit was fully out of his cave.

"Okay, I'll talk to Petey," Twain said. He was standing nearly behind her and she had a terrible urge to turn and lean back into his tall, hard chest. It would be so much more comfortable—and warmer—than the hard oak spindles of her stool.

As if reading her mind, Twain moved even closer to her and placed a hand on her shoulder.

Suddenly Liv didn't care that she was in a local bar in her hometown with people who undoubtedly knew her family—or at the very least knew the Bad Luck Beck Brothers. She twisted slightly and leaned back. In a mini "trust game," she waited to see if Twain would catch her. When she felt the warmth of his chest

at her back, she rested not only her weight on him but also her…
soul, or something close to it.

Twain's warm hand melted into her shoulder, and he gave the
smallest of squeezes.

She might have imagined it, but she thought she saw Deni
send Twain an "I told you so" look.

Twenty-Three

"AT FIRST I WAS THINKING IT WOULD BE A CIRCULAR bar, but Deni just gave me a layout that would work better for that area. See? An L-shaped bar gives us more room over here." Petey Ryan pointed to the plans that sat on the table in front of them at the Cat's Meow.

"Is she coming?" Twain asked.

Petey checked his watch. "She wasn't sure she could make it. She was going to try, but she told me to tell you to call her if you had any questions about specs and such."

"So, you have a liquor license? For sure?"

Petey took a sip of his beer. "Not yet. But I've got a good lead on one. Either way, if your schedule is as tight as you say, let's get it done now to have it in when we open. If we use it for just pop and food for now, so be it."

"Okay," Twain said.

"Really? Okay? You're in? For sure?"

Twain nodded and took a drink of his beer, the golden liquid going down easily after a long day in the woods.

And another evening not spent with Liv.

He loved his son and was happy Matt was home from Florida, but it had been impossible to find time for Twain to be alone with Liv in the two weeks since Matt had returned. And so they hadn't been able to resume their baby-making practices.

"I'm in. I've got a piece of wood in mind, a burl from a tiger maple. Matt and I are harvesting it tomorrow and then I can work on the bar during the evenings for you." Why not? It wasn't like his evenings were being spent in Liv's bed anymore. Might as well keep his hands busy in other ways.

"I appreciate, it, Twain. I really do. I know it's something I can just forget about with you and know it's going to be done right. Kind of like with Deni and Sawyer."

"It ain't gonna be cheap," he said with a grin, which his old buddy returned.

"Nothing good ever is. Again, kind of like with Deni and Sawyer."

They toasted to their joint project and drank as they went over the layout for the bar area that Deni had come up with for Petey.

"There's this burl that I was thinking might work in the middle of a circular bar, but I'm starting to think it could create a really cool effect right where the corners come together." He pointed to the plans, and Petey nodded.

"I'm not even going to ask what a burl is, that's how much I trust you," he said.

Twain laughed and sat back in his chair, bringing his beer bottle with him, resting it on his chest as he stretched out his legs.

He ran through the timeline in his mind of doing this project for Petey. Logging in the summer was not nearly as productive as in the winter because the ground could be unpredictable in its softness, causing delays and postponements if using the large equipment became impossible or unsafe. He'd need probably a couple of weeks if he worked on Petey's project in the evenings. By the time he had all the wood from Toivo's land cut, loaded, and ready for the mill, it would be near the end of April.

And hopefully Liv would be pregnant.

As seemed to happen in the past three weeks since he and Liv had started...trying, when Twain thought about an impending pregnancy, he was filled with warring emotions.

On one hand, he had grown more and more excited with the

idea of having another child and couldn't wait for it to actually happen. Now, not only at ease with the idea, Twain found himself thinking of baby names and mentally rearranging things in his home so he'd be able to turn the spare room into a baby's room when the time came.

On the other hand (okay, maybe a different appendage) was the dread of knowing that once Liv was indeed pregnant, there would be no more reason for their conjugal visits.

But surely, once they knew she was pregnant and had told Matt, Twain would become more involved in her life. He could help with creating a nursery for her. Finish off the basement and move her office down there.

Be like a...family.

An ache in Twain's chest, one that had been close to the surface since that night in Liv's shower, twined its way past his heart and into his mouth as he said to Petey, "You said that night you were here with Zeke that you'd only been in love twice, and it was with the same woman."

Petey nodded. He looked closely at Twain, but he didn't seem surprised by Twain's abrupt change of subject. "Yep. My Alison. We were in high school the first time. Shit happened and we...we weren't ready then."

"Huh," Twain said, digesting his friend's words. "But you are now?"

"Without a doubt."

"Did you both change that much? Is that why it works now?"

While Petey seemed to think about Twain's question, Twain's memory flashed back to the early days of being with Liv.

He'd been through the grinder with Jenny Korpii, his girlfriend of two years, having broken up with her a few months before he took Liv home from Paula Ilonen's party.

Jenny had been high maintenance and had wrung him out. Twain, in his youthful innocence, had mistaken the volatility of their relationship for passion. When he'd first started seeing Liv, he was struck by her no-nonsense attitude. No demands, no questions on whom he was with or where he was going. She was happy to be with Twain, no matter what.

She was clingy, but not in a possessive way that irritated him. No, hers was a quiet, soft clinginess that he'd found he'd liked at the time.

By the end of their marriage, he'd found it exhausting, but that hadn't been Liv's fault.

Now, there was none of that. She still desired him, which was easy enough to see. And hear…as she moaned her release. And feel…when she'd shatter in his arms.

But though the desire was still there, and Twain would guess the love she'd felt for him was there too, there was no sense of desperation about her. No fear. No cling of any kind.

And though the stupid nineteen-year-old in him might feel a bit miffed about that fact, the adult in Twain couldn't be more happy.

Finally…*finally*, it felt like a true partnership with Liv, not just him trying to make her feel secure and her trying to let go of her fear of losing him.

Except, so far, their partnership was only for the purposes of another baby.

But could it be more?

Maybe it wasn't about Liv changing at all, but about Twain changing, growing. He'd never been remotely close to falling for anyone since Liv. Was there a reason for that? Was it less about the changes in her, and more about him finally maturing enough to fully love a woman in an equal, adult way?

He'd thought he'd manned up when Liv was pregnant, but apparently there was much more to it than just doing the right thing. You had to let yourself be open to love. Had he done that? Was he able to do that now?

"I'm not sure it's that we changed as much as it is that we're finally just ready for each other, you know?"

Twain wasn't looking at Petey as he nodded. "Yeah, I think I do."

Petey got up and walked to the bar while Twain thought about what Petey had said. Could Twain and Liv just finally be ready for each other?

When Petey returned from the bar with two fresh bottles of beer, Twain took one from him and set it on the table.

"You know," Petey said, "there are a lot of parallels between Alison and me and you and Liv."

Twain could have sworn that he hadn't mentioned Liv's name once during the evening.

"Come on," Petey said. "It's me. You can't get nothin' past me."

Twain finished off his beer and then switched it out for the full one, taking a healthy slug. "Jesus. What are you even talking about?" He was about to deny thinking about Liv but found he didn't want to. "Parallels how?"

Petey smirked, knowing he'd fished something out of Twain he hadn't been willing to give up. "We both got together young. Fell hard." He looked over at Twain. "Well, I did. And I know Liv did for you."

Twain coughed a little and waved for Petey to continue.

"We, Al and I, got ourselves into a little…situation. Not unlike you and Liv…" He gave Twain a pointed look.

Holy shit. Petey had knocked up Alison Jukuri in high school? But…obviously there was no kid now.

"Oh," he said, figuring it out. He had no judgment on Petey and Alison's choice back then. But for him, the thought had never even entered his mind.

"It wasn't… We didn't… Oh, hell, it doesn't matter now how it all played out. Just know that a year later when you had to leave school to marry Liv and have Matty, I had, I don't know, very mixed feelings about it."

"I had no idea."

"Nobody did. Nobody *does*." He gave another pointed look, his large body suddenly seeming even larger. "Nobody *will*."

Twain crossed his beer bottle over his heart. "No worries. It's safe with me."

Petey seemed to relax, sitting back in his chair.

"So anyway, in a weird way, I was jealous of you back then. But in other ways, it felt like I'd dodged a bullet, you know?"

"Sure, that's natural."

"And then when I heard about you and Liv splitting up...I don't know. It really bothered me. I kind of projected myself into the situation. That maybe Al and I wouldn't have made it, either."

Twain took in a deep breath and let it out. Even though Petey had just told him something very private, and apparently something very secret, there was no way Twain was going to spill the details of the end with Liv.

He hadn't then, when it would have mattered, and he wasn't going to now.

"Marriage is hard," he said. "Even with everything in your favor, let alone being young, broke, and having a baby."

"Yeah," Petey agreed.

Twain wondered if Petey, clairvoyant as he seemed to be, also saw another parallel between the two couples. "So, when you saw Alison again recently and spent time with her, you just, what, *knew?*"

"Kind of. I mean, I saw her all the time, in the summers and stuff. Kind of like how you always saw Liv...because of Matt."

"Riiiight..." Twain said, suspicious of where Petey was going. Could he possibly know?

"But then we spent a lot of time together in close quarters after I had my knee surgery."

If the close quarters they'd been in were anything like what he and Liv had been doing, no wonder Petey was crowing about being so happy and in love.

"Yeah?" Twain said, leaning forward, curious.

"And I realized that I was crazy in love with her. Simple as that."

Twain sat back in his seat, somewhat disappointed. Somehow, he'd thought there'd be more to it. "Oh."

Petey reached across the table and knocked Twain's baseball cap off his head. "Don't 'oh' me. It's a big deal, being in love. Especially for a guy like me."

"I know," Twain said, leaning over to retrieve his hat.

"Do you? Do you know what it's like to finally be in love—again, or for the first time—at our age?"

This time with Liv was so different—his feelings, their circumstances. The only thing that was the same was the great connection they had in bed. His feelings for her felt very new and fresh, almost raw.

Was Twain in love with Liv?

Finally?

Twenty-Four

GOD, SHE WAS SUCH A FOOL. AS IF NOT KISSING TWAIN while they were scorching up the sheets (and the shower, and the floor, etc.) was going to protect her heart.

When it had only left her wanting more.

And, as she stared at the negative on the pregnancy test stick, she realized that's exactly what she was going to get. More. More Twain. More of his big body wrapped around hers.

Which, as consolation prizes went, wasn't a bad one.

After burying the test in her bathroom trash—though Matty never used her bathroom—she washed up, splashing water on what suspiciously looked like tears, and made her way into the kitchen.

Shockingly, Matty was already up and dressed, an empty bowl of cereal on the table and sandwich ingredients on the counter.

Saturday in the forest with Twain. Right. Matty didn't get up this early, and on his own, for school.

Zombie-like, she squeezed her son's shoulder as she passed him and poured herself a cup of the coffee that he'd had the good graces to have already made.

Taking her mug to the table, she watched her son make two—no, three—sandwiches for his day. No more PB&J. Her son had become a salami and mustard man.

Man. Not quite, but nearly there.

He was so like his father in his movements. Liv felt her throat closing up with a wash of desperate love for her little boy who was little no longer.

Life moved so fast. She thought of the years she'd lost with Twain, years that they could have been a family. And for what? Pride?

Yes, that pride had made her the woman she was now—and she liked that woman.

But would she have traded just some of that pride and taken Twain back if she'd known how much she would miss him?

Funny, she didn't know how terribly she'd missed him for the past seven years until he was back in her life.

And suddenly, she knew she didn't want that for her son.

"Matty?" she said, clearing her throat, having not spoken since she woke.

"Matt," he corrected her, though there was no teenage scorn in his voice, and he kept on making his lunch.

"Matt," she said. "About Heather Summers…"

"God, I told you, nothing happened. We just went over there because—"

"No, that's not what I meant," she interrupted him. He looked up from his task at her, leery of her next words, his body already tensing. "I just want to…take back, I guess, what I said when we were driving home from Marquette."

"What was that?" he asked, but she knew from his body language that he vividly remembered her warning.

"About protecting your heart. About being the one who loves the most being…well…that it…"

"Sucks," he finished for her.

She nodded and took a sip from her coffee. Setting the mug back on the table, sitting in the same spot where she'd sat across from Twain every morning for a week, she cradled the warm cup in her hands, hoping the heat would seep into her bones.

Into her soul.

"Yeah, it sucks." Remembering her mission, she shook her head a little and looked at her son, who was studying her. "It *can* suck, absolutely. But sometimes it's better to be the one who loves. Sometimes it gives you a…clarity about things."

She could tell he didn't want to be talking about such things with his mother of all people, and yet he leaned on the island and said, "In what way clarity? Wouldn't it just plain suck?"

She took a deep breath and let it out. How to explain this when she didn't fully understand it herself, even after all these years.

"If you love, and it's a true love, there is no better feeling in the world," she said cautiously.

Sandwiches abandoned, Matty pinned her with his eyes. "Even if they don't love you back?"

"Yes, even then. It hurts, believe me, and if you let it, it can eat you up. The knowledge of it. The fuming about the injustice of it. The wondering what you could do differently…better… more." She looked out the window at the sun breaking through the April clouds. "But there's also a…pureness to it. You're not in love with them solely because of how they feel. It's hard to explain, really." Which kind of surprised her—her love for Twain had been such a constant for so long it seemed like she should be able to speak more eloquently about it.

"I guess what I'm trying to say—badly—is if you love someone more than they love you, it can suck sometimes, sure. But it can also be a very rare gift—love so strong that it doesn't need the other's love to grow and thrive."

He nodded slowly, seeming to think about it, his eyes still on Liv. She shrugged. "Besides, protecting your heart doesn't work anyway. I was wrong to tell you to try it."

His eyes grew big, and he opened his mouth to speak. Liv steeled herself for the questions sure to come. Mainly about Liv's heart not being protected.

She was literally saved by the bell as the front doorbell rang, with Twain coming to collect Matty.

"I'll get it," she said, rising from the table, wrapping her robe tighter around herself, as if for protection. Ha! Just when she'd admitted—to herself and her son—that such a thing wasn't possible.

"Finish your sandwiches. I'll clean up the stuff," she directed, and started to leave the kitchen.

"Thanks, Mom," Matty said, and from the look he gave her, she knew he meant for more than just KP duty.

"Anytime," she said, walking to the foyer where Twain's big silhouette showed through the glass portions of the front door.

"Hi," she said as she opened the door, stepping back to let him enter.

Since their week together, Twain had started coming to the front door to collect and drop off Matty, where before he usually waited in the truck unless they had something specific to discuss about schedules or finances.

"What's wrong?" Twain said once he was in the door.

Did it show? Yes, to Twain it probably did, though no one else would likely notice.

"Negative," she said, softly so Matty wouldn't be able to hear in the kitchen.

"Shit," he said, just as quietly. His expression fleetingly made her feel better; he was truly as upset about it as she was. And it wasn't just that misery loved company, but more the fact that Twain was also disappointed that they weren't pregnant yet.

He wanted this baby, too.

His eyes flicked toward the kitchen, and she nodded that yes, Matty was in there. Twain stepped closer to her and said, "But you said it might be a false negative this early, right? That at two weeks it could show negative and then a week or two later, positive?"

"Yes," she said. "But—"

"Okay, I've got everything," Matty said, coming around the corner. Twain made the movement away from her look smooth, like he had been on his way to get Matty and had stopped.

She did notice Matty look between her and Twain for a second more than usual, but that could have just been because of the talk she and Matty had just had.

"Have a good day, guys," she said. Surprisingly, Matty bent over and kissed her cheek. "Thanks, Mom," he said, meeting her eyes.

"You're welcome," she said. "Remember, your dad will drop you off at the restaurant for your uncle's birthday dinner." To Twain, she said, "You're sure you don't mind?"

Twain shook his head. "Nope. I'll be going back to Calumet anyway. It's on my way. Which brother?"

"Joe," she said. "My parents just got back from Florida a couple of days ago. You should come in and join us. They'd love to see you." Twain arched a brow at her. "Well, Joe would love to see you, at least," she said. Her sisters? Not so much. They weren't big Twain fans after the divorce and the subsequent years.

"We'll see," Twain said, which was pretty much a no. Liv didn't blame him.

Matty and Twain walked out of her house, and she stood in the open doorway watching them walk away from her. About halfway to the truck, Twain pulled on Matty's arm, stopping him. He handed Matty the keys, said something Liv couldn't hear, and then turned and started walking back to the house. Matty watched for a second and then continued on to the truck, entering the driver's side.

"Did you forget something?" Liv said, wondering what it would be that Twain came back for as opposed to Matty.

"No," Twain said, closing the door behind him. He took her hand, leading her out of the view of the door windows, and then pulled her into his arms, enveloping her in a warm hug.

"I'm sorry it was negative, Liv," he said. She burrowed into him, letting her tears of disappointment fall, rubbing her cheeks into his big work jacket. Feeling a soft kiss on the top of her head, she wrapped her arms tighter around his waist.

She could have stayed that way for hours, taking the comfort Twain was offering. But Matty was out in the truck, and they had work to do. Finally, she pulled away and wiped her eyes.

"Like you said, it might still end up being a positive. I'll wait a week and take another test."

Twain nodded. "And if not, we'll just keep trying." There was no question in his voice, and she found she had no voice of her own, so she only nodded.

"You'll be okay?" he softly asked.

She nodded and then led him to the door. "Go. Be manly. Cut things down."

He looked at her closely, and she gave him a wobbly smile. Satisfied, he nodded, turned, and walked out of the door.

She closed it after him, walked down the hallway, and got back into bed.

Twenty-Five

"AND REMEMBER, YOU NEVER TRY TO HARVEST A BURL from a tree unless you're absolutely sure you won't kill the tree. Unless, of course, the whole tree is coming down, like this one was."

"I know, Dad," Matty said, with the long-suffering sigh of a teenager. He walked around the tiger maple, which they'd moved to a cleared area behind the T&B offices. "You've told me a thousand times."

Had he? He knew he drummed safety and conservationism into Matt every chance he got, but Twain wasn't sure how much Matt retained. Being a logger was about more than cutting down trees, or at least it should be. It was about making sure you were cutting responsibly, taking into account regrowth and even strengthening of forests with strategic planning and harvesting.

Sustainability was a buzzword that got a lot of play, but it had been important to Twain since his forestry classes at Tech, and also from Eddie showing him how to do the least damage and the most good within Mother Nature's temple.

He loved the woods, felt at peace there as he did nowhere else, and it seemed that Matt felt the same way. Twain wanted to instill the same sense of responsibility in Matt that Eddie had in Twain. Not only was it the right thing to do, but one day T&B would belong to Matt, and Twain wanted him to be ready.

He watched as his son studied the burl from different angles, coming up with a harvesting plan. Twain took his coffee and lowered himself into one of the stump chairs that he and Sawyer had sat on just over a month ago.

What a month it had been. Twain now had to consider that his business might not be left solely to Matt but also to his and Liv's newest child.

Then he remembered the negative test of this morning, and a deep sadness overcame him. If he was feeling this disconsolate, he could only imagine the day Liv was having.

"I think the burl is too deep to salvage the rest of the tree in one piece," Matt said, looking to Twain for his opinion. Twain nodded, as he'd already surmised the same thing. "I mean, maybe you'd be able to salvage six inches or so beneath it, but then you risk damaging the burl," Matt added.

A sharp sense of pride cut into Twain, helping to alleviate— at least for a moment—the sadness he'd been feeling since talking with Liv. "Exactly," he said. "So, what should you do? How are you going to proceed?"

Matt studied the whole felled tree, which was nearly twenty feet long, the burl about halfway up. Twain could see his son mentally measuring, looking at the areas below the burl and above. Finally, Matt shrugged and turned to Twain. "It's not good. We're not going to be able to have either side be long enough to make good lumber."

Twain nodded. Again, Matt's thoughts matched his own. "So, what's the answer?" Matt looked at the tree and then came over to join Twain.

Standing, Twain was still taller than Matt, though he wasn't sure how much longer that would be true. But sitting down, with Matt towering over him, Twain realized again how much of a man his son was quickly becoming. "Well, you've already got plans for the burl, right? You're going to use it for Petey Ryan's bar? So, cut the burl and use the rest for something else."

"And what if I hadn't already made plans for the burl? What would you do then?"

"I'd do a cost analysis on what I could get for the burl versus what the longer lumber would bring in."

"Right. Exactly," Twain said, pride again swelling in his chest.

There were lots of other factors in making those types of decisions, such as finding someone who would pay top dollar for the burl (which was sometimes easy, sometimes not), the going rate at the mill for top-grade tiger maple, and other basic supply-and-demand-type stuff. But Matt studying the profitability of the options as the answer was how a businessman should think. Hell, even using the term "cost analysis" thrilled Twain to no end.

He was good at this. Being a father to Matt. And he found himself hoping like hell that he'd get the chance to do it again.

Maybe it really was too soon and the test had showed a false negative. Or maybe they'd just have to keep trying.

As Matt donned his safety goggles and set about cutting the tree on either side of the burl, Twain let his thoughts travel down the road of the possible logistics in getting Liv alone now that Matt was back, Tech was in session, and Twain was again able to be in the forest for long days.

A level of frustration that he'd had since Matt had returned and Liv and he had to return to just polite co-parents burned in Twain's gut.

Liv had told him in Marquette that she wasn't interested in Twain for anything more than being the father to her child. No desire to get back together, no ulterior motives. And he absolutely believed her. Their marriage hadn't been perfect, but Liv had never lied to him, and he didn't think she'd start now.

Not perfect, no, but their marriage—at least until the end—had been good. Nice. Comfortable. And the week with Liv had driven home to Twain how much he'd missed married life. Missed being a family.

Missed Liv.

Would it be so bad to explore the notion of getting back together while they were having sex? The thought itself was kind of a ludicrous version of cart before the horse, but Twain couldn't stop thinking about it.

And what would he say to Matt? *Hey, son. Your mom and I are going to start dating. And we might also be having another baby.* How confusing would that be for a kid?

Although when (he refused to think in "ifs") they did get pregnant, there would be talks with Matt that would be confusing anyway.

So was it all or nothing? Either completely back together or just getting pregnant? Dating didn't seem like an option to him, for some reason. It would be all in for Twain. He missed her and their life together, but it was more than that.

She had become…more to him.

There had been changes in her, for sure. A self-confidence that her knitting business—or perhaps just life—had given her. And it was damn attractive.

And he must have changed too, in the past seven years. He'd realized that you needed to protect what you valued, to treasure what you have, and to always, always help it grow.

Sustainability was needed in life and relationships as much as in the forest, or it would all be barren fields of nothing but stumps. Which is kind of what his life had been without Liv.

"There," Matt said, the chainsaw coming to a stop as he stood back from the tree. Twain stood and surveyed his son's work.

"Really good work," he said, patting Matt's back. "Let's take a lunch break and then we'll load the burl onto the front loader and bring it in to the shop."

"I can't wait to see what it looks like inside."

Twain walked around to the other side, where the burl had been separated from the tree. "If the remnants around it are any guess, it's going to be a beauty." He gave the burl a push with his boot, barely moving the large wooden boulder. "Man, that's got to weigh nearly a hundred pounds." Some of the woodworkers Twain had dealt with in the past would pay up to two hundred dollars a pound for a maple burl of this size. He'd probably made a mistake by using it in Petey Ryan's project, but Twain liked the idea of it staying in the Copper Country.

"It's going to be really cool as part of the bar," Matt said, echoing Twain's thoughts.

They ate lunch silently, gobbling their sandwiches, and then Twain let Matt load the burl up and bring it to the shop, where together they struggled to lift it onto a worktable.

"We'll have to wait to put the lathe to it," Twain said, "It's getting late."

"But you'll wait until I'm here with you?" Matt asked.

"Yep, come on."

On the drive to Calumet, Twain took the opportunity to bring up Matt's crush (hookup? God, he hoped not) with Heather Summers.

"Man, what is with you two? Do you text each other when it's 'Let's talk to Matt' day?"

"You and your mom talk about this today?"

"Yeah, and—well, no, not exactly. That's what I thought she wanted to talk about, but it wasn't really."

Twain drove on, waiting. He wanted to ask what they'd discussed, but didn't want to push. He could tell Matt was debating whether to say anything or not. Just as they were nearing the Calumet Village line, Matt said, "Mom seemed sad this morning."

Twain kept his hands on the wheel and his eyes on the road, but said, "Yeah, to me too. That's why I went back inside, to see if she was okay."

"And do you think she was? Okay?"

"Yeah, I do. I think it was just a case of the blues. We can all get them this time of year. It's the long winters. Just a bit of cabin fever."

Matt looked nervously over at him. "But not like Deni, right? Not *that* kind of blues?"

"No, not that kind." Twain reached over and gave Matt's shoulder a squeeze. "Just a blah day. I'll bet she'll be fine when you see her at the party."

Matt looked at him for reassurance, which Twain tried to convey, hoping that his words were true.

While Matt had been away, it'd been easy. But their son was smart, and he was already catching on that something was amiss with Liv. It seemed all the more important to Twain to have some definition of his relationship with Liv sooner rather than later. Twain wasn't sure he'd be able to hide his burgeoning feelings around his ex-wife.

And suddenly, he didn't want to.

"Let's get to my place and get cleaned up. I think I will stop in at your uncle's party for a while and say happy birthday to Joe."

Twenty-Six

WHEN TWAIN FIRST ENTERED KOSKELA'S KITCHEN, LIV thought it was to just let her know that he was dropping Matt off or to make plans for a future drop-off or pick-up. But when he walked toward her, the gleam in his eye told her that he'd come to the family party for more than that.

Closed for Joe's party, the restaurant was filled with her family. With all the nieces and nephews, that was pretty much the same number as a packed dinner rush.

"Hey," he said when he reached her. "Hey, Joe! Happy birthday," he said to her brother, whom she'd been standing with near the swinging metal doors that led to the kitchen.

"Hey, Twain! Thanks for stopping by," Joe said, shaking Twain's hand. Her younger brother and Twain had always gotten along well and had kept up a distant friendship over the years. Which was more than anyone else in her family had done.

"How was your day?" Liv asked Twain. Matty had gotten sucked up by her parents and her sisters, who had pretty much parted like the Red Sea when Twain had entered. He'd made a point of nodding to them all and saying hi as he'd walked by.

"Good. He was just…outstanding today. Really made some good choices with the wood." She could see the pride in Twain's face, and she couldn't help but smile back at him.

"How are *you* doing?" he asked. His voice didn't give anything away, but she knew what he was asking.

"I'm doing good. A nap and a long shower did the trick, and I'm feeling much better, thanks."

"Are you sick?" Joe asked.

Shaking her head, she said, "I thought I might be coming down with something, but I feel fine now."

Joe looked back and forth between them, then shrugged and asked Twain something about the Red Wings. Their chances for the Cup, or something. Liv pretty much tuned them out and just stared at Twain as he chatted with her brother. Stared and desperately racked her mind to try to figure out how and when they could try again.

"You have a minute to talk?" Twain asked when his conversation with Joe wound down. She nodded.

"Apparently, I'm being summoned to cut the cake," Joe said. "Stick around," he said to Twain, and then left.

Twain started to say something, but her family had started singing "Happy Birthday" and it was hard to hear. She should have joined in, but a weird sense of urgency overtook her. She wanted—needed—to hear what Twain wanted to talk about right now, not sing to her brother, who had a pained look on his face at all the attention.

"Let's go in here," she said, taking Twain's hand and leading him through the light swinging doors and into the kitchen. She stopped a few steps in, leaning against the stainless steel prep area. "What's up?"

He stepped close to her. Very close to her. God, was he thinking of a quickie in her family's restaurant?

And why was she suddenly thinking of ways to make it happen?

"Umm...yeah..." he said. She watched his Adam's apple bounce in his strong neck. The singing had stopped from behind the doors, and the buzz and hum of distant conversations came through. "I was just wondering if, maybe, we could... If maybe we should..."

Twain at a loss for words, looking...was it...vulnerable?

What on earth did he want to ask her? She was already sleeping with him and planned on continuing until she was pregnant. He had to know that one negative test was not an end for her, no matter how sad she'd been this morning.

An old tingly feeling, one she hadn't felt for years and years, crept up her back.

Hope.

Was Twain going to ask for more? Was that why he was looking at her so intently, with a hunger that she hadn't seen in his eyes since they'd first started dating?

And then years of the Pet Rock knocking any hope out of her came full circle.

Maybe he wanted out completely? Maybe he wasn't even willing to be her child's father any longer?

The voices from beyond turned to a low-level hum, and in a startling moment of clarity, she realized that she would no longer bow down to the Pet Rock. She hadn't lived in fear of losing Twain in seven years. She had, in fact, lived just fine without him, and she would again, no matter what he was going to say to her.

Hope. Yes, hope. It was a good feeling, even if she only cautiously let it in.

"I think we—" Twain's voice was cut off by a conversation between her sisters Laura and Robin as they came to stand on the other side of the doors.

"Looks like he left while we were singing," Laura said. Liv could see the tops of their blond heads through the little circular window on the door, but they weren't tall enough to see into the kitchen to know that Liv and Twain were right behind them.

"Good. I hope he didn't upset Liv."

"I don't see her. She didn't leave too, did she?"

"No, there's Matty. Maybe she walked Twain to his truck or something," Robin said.

There was a pause, and Liv looked up at Twain, who was looking down at her, waiting for the women to leave. If they could hear them so clearly, surely they would be able to hear him if he spoke.

"He looks good, though. I hate to say it, but he does."

"He sure does, eh?"

Liv felt heat rush over her as Twain continued to look down at her. Just a hint of a grin quirked up at the corners of his mouth, and she gave him an "Oh, brother" look. She'd never live down the fact that her sisters—who basically ignored him any chance they got—thought he was good looking.

"Hardly seems fair, but he keep getting better looking as he ages."

"Right, not fair," Robin said. Both women sighed, and Twain's grin went to full-blown smirk. Liv placed a hand on his chest and shook her head.

"Too bad he's just another cheating bastard," Laura said. Liv felt Twain's muscles tense under her hand, which she let drop away like she'd been burned.

"Poor Liv," Laura said.

"Yeah, poor Liv," Robin agreed. "Dad, don't lift that by yourself. John, help Dad get…" The words got softer and out of hearing range as her sisters moved away from the doors.

It took forever for Liv to look back up at Twain, and when she did, it was almost a physical blow to see the look of hurt and anger on his face.

"Poor Liv. Poor, saintly Liv, who had to put up with that dog, Twain." He moved closer to her, pinning her against the table. He bent his head, and she could feel his breath hot against her neck. "But we both know the truth, don't we?" He nudged her hair, his lips against her neck. She could have fooled herself and called it a kiss, but it wasn't. Right now, Twain was much more likely to bite her than kiss her. "Don't we?" he whispered in her ear.

Hope was gone. Pet Rock was back.

"Yes," she whispered back, the sound barely leaving her mouth. But he heard her. And even if he hadn't, he could have sensed her answer by the defeat that rocked through her body.

"Yeah," he said. He backed up enough for him to look down

at her. God, she used to love when he'd tower over her, standing so close, looking down at her. Even moments ago, it had been so sexy.

"I know what we agreed to say when we split up. I know I'm the one who was adamant," he said.

"That's right, you were. I wanted..." But she didn't go on. Twain had made the rule on this seven years ago, and she had gone along with it, even though she knew it would hurt them both.

"And that's okay; what people say behind my back," he said in a voice that contradicted his words. "But we both know I never cheated on you, Liv."

She hung her head, but his fingers touched the bottom of her chin, lifting it and forcing her to look at him. She could have closed her eyes, but she wasn't that much of a coward. Not anymore. She had changed from the woman who agreed to let Twain be the fall guy for their marriage blowing up.

She lifted her head higher, meeting his eyes. "No, Twain. You never cheated on me. I was the one who cheated."

She thought she'd see victory on his rugged face, but there was none. Instead, she saw pain and confusion, even after all these years. She opened her mouth to say more, but his fingers slid up from her chin to cover her lips. He shook his head.

Not able to look at him any longer, having used all her nerve in her admission, she now hung her head and watched his feet as he turned around and walked out of the kitchen.

Just like he'd walked away from her all those years ago.

Just like she'd asked him to.

Twenty-Seven

Seven Years Ago

"SO? ANOTHER DRINK?" GUTHRIE PRINCE ASKED LIV AT lunch. But he wasn't really asking her if she wanted another drink, and they both knew it.

Months of skirting the attentions of the visiting professor had finally come to this moment of truth.

In a way, Liv had made her decision when she'd accepted his lunch invitation, even though he'd asked her every Friday for the past two months. When this morning she'd finally agreed, he'd nearly choked on his coffee before looking at her with his charming smile and penetrating blue eyes. "You're sure?" he asked at the time, and Liv had known exactly what he was asking her.

"Yes," she'd said.

"Yes," she said now to the offer of another drink.

They had the afternoon off. The Psychology department at Tech was closed so the faculty could attend a seminar in Green Bay. Guthrie, being on faculty for only a semester, and Liv, being staff, not faculty, had stayed behind. There were others in the office who hadn't gone, but they'd all cleared out at noon, it being the end of the semester. Liv had remained to finish up some paperwork for the dean.

Now they sat at the Indian River Steak House, drinking vodka tonics (a first for Liv) and barely touching their salads as

Guthrie regaled her with stories of academic life in his native Scotland.

She'd been married to Twain for eight years, loved him more than the world. But at twenty-seven, she was receiving from Guthrie a look of intense desire that she'd never seen on Twain's face.

And God help her, it felt so good.

The compliments, the flirting, the semester of being secretly pursued had been flattering, but it was more than that. It had touched Liv in a way that her love for Twain never had.

The semester was over, the farewell event for Guthrie held last night due to the faculty being gone today. When they said their goodbyes after lunch, Liv would never see him again.

Which was why she'd said yes to lunch. Why she said yes to another drink.

And why she would say yes to what he would surely suggest next.

He did, in smooth Scottish tones with a gentle wag of the brow that she found charming, though she knew it was well used.

"My place. Follow me," she said when they were in the parking lot and he offered to show her the apartment he'd been in, which was now mostly packed up.

During the drive home, she was in a fog, several times almost taking a wrong turn to lead Guthrie away from her apartment. Their apartment—hers and Twain's.

Inside, he took her in his arms and kissed her soundly and deeply, and her mind tried to inventory the differences between his kisses and Twain's. But thinking about Twain killed everything, and she wanted—just for a tiny moment—to be more than the wife that Twain didn't love.

She wanted to have a man stare at her as Guthrie was now. A man to undress her with reverence and delight, exclaiming how beautiful she was and how much he wanted her. A man who held her hand against his erection and told her that she'd been driving him crazy since the moment he first laid eyes on her.

Someone who laid her down on the bed and stared at her with hunger in his eyes, all while reciting her favorable attributes and all the things he wanted to do to her.

They were words and looks that she'd desired for so long, and that she'd never had from Twain. And even though she loved Twain and had no lasting feelings for Guthrie beyond how he was making her feel at that exact moment, she couldn't deny how starved she'd been for this kind of attention.

As he kissed her body all over, she begged him to keep talking, to keep saying how much he wanted her. She needed that, so she would know that being so desperately wanted by a man was possible, so she could, in some small, small way, justify this to herself.

And then she opened her eyes. Instead of Twain's green eyes looking at her, it was Guthrie's blue gaze, and suddenly, everything felt terribly, terribly wrong.

His touch, which moments ago was tantalizing and dangerous, now seemed like sandpaper on her skin. His kiss, warm and passionate before, was now harsh and cold. His words, hot and tempting, now seemed tawdry and vulgar.

"Guthrie," she said, her hand on his shoulder as he bent to kiss her again. "I think I've made a mistake." He was leaning over her, his head propped up, elbow on the bed. His shirt was unbuttoned and open. Liv vaguely remembered unbuttoning it as he led her down the hallway of their small apartment. His hand was on her bare tummy, skimming the waistband of her panties.

"Ah, lass, but we're having so much fun. And ye know how bonny I think ye are." His accent was laid on thicker than she'd heard it before, and the...the...*fakeness* of the whole situation doused any flames of passion, as if she'd jumped in Lake Superior after a sauna.

"No, Guthrie," she said, rising to sit. "I can't. I'm sorry."

He didn't rise, letting his hand slide as she rose so that it rested on her thigh. "I'm sorry to hear that, darling."

Fake. The word echoed in her head.

No, Twain had never declared undying love. He'd never ripped the buttons on her top trying to get it off in his haste to touch her breasts. He'd never told her that she was precious and lovely and he couldn't wait to be inside her.

Her husband didn't love her.

But what he *did* feel for her was real. And true. And quiet, yes, but no less satisfying than what little she'd done with Guthrie. More so, because, of course, she was very much in love with her husband.

So what the hell was she doing next to a half-dressed Scotsman?

"What's going on?" Someone had spoken her exact thoughts out loud. She wanted to say, "I know, right?" but wasn't sure to whom. It didn't appear that Guthrie had said anything. But when she looked in his eyes, she saw they weren't looking at her any longer, but rather over her shoulder.

Before she turned, her confused mind registered that it had been Twain who'd spoken.

"Twain," she said. "It's not what you think." God, were those the most clichéd words ever, or what? And yet, in this particular instance, Liv felt that they were true.

He stood there, his eyes going from her, in only her bra and panties, over to Guthrie, and then back to her. She waited for Twain to explode, for his years of decking people on the ice to surface. She rose on her knees to come between Twain and Guthrie if needed (though, God, she hoped it wouldn't be—Twain could snap Guthrie like a twig), but Twain never made a move. He just stood there in the doorway.

"Twain," she said softly. "It's—" The look on his face stopped her.

There had been shock at first and then anger. Both so understandable, and both filling Liv with self-loathing.

But then…there. That. She knew she hadn't imagined it. The emotion that played across her husband's face, the one he couldn't hide, the one that ran the deepest.

Relief.

Something deep inside Liv's soul cracked. Opening the same gaping hole that she momentarily—and idiotically—thought could be filled by loving attention, even from another man. She sank down on her haunches. Defeated.

She hadn't planned this—Twain finding her with Guthrie. He never came home during the day when he was working. She'd never in a million years want Twain to walk in on her with another man. But now that it had happened, a bright light was shining on her worst fear.

Her husband not only didn't love her but was relieved that their marriage was over.

"Get out, Twain," she said quietly. So quietly both Twain and Guthrie leaned toward her, as if they couldn't believe their ears. She wasn't so sure about what she'd said, either. But on some level, she knew what she had to do. For herself as well as Twain. "Please, Twain. I want you to leave."

Shock. If there was still relief, he hid it now. A quick nod, and he walked out of the bedroom. Seconds later, she heard the front door slam. She got rid of Guthrie moments later.

And tried to figure out how she wanted to live the rest of her life.

Twenty-Eight

Seven Years Ago

"ARE YOU IN LOVE WITH HIM?" TWAIN ASKED LIV TWO
nights after he'd walked in on his wife in bed—*his* bed!—with
another man. Since leaving the apartment, Twain had crashed
on the lumpy, beat-up loveseat in the Tuisku Logging offices.
He'd called Liv that afternoon and asked her to bring Matt to
her mother's for the night so they could have the apartment to
themselves. Now he sat with Liv at their kitchen table, wanting to
understand what the hell was going on.

Liv cheating on him? It just didn't make sense. And yet,
somewhere in the very dark place in the very back of his head, it
kind of did.

You drove her to this.

But he needed to know where they stood. He couldn't spend
another night in this limbo.

"God, no. I'm not in love with him," Liv said strongly, as if
the mere thought that she might be in love with the guy she was
sleeping with was absurd. Twain stayed silent, and she went on.
"Nothing like that."

"Were there other times? How long has it been going on?"

"It hasn't been 'going on.' And it wasn't even that one time,
the other day. Not really."

"Looked pretty real to me."

"I mean we didn't even... It didn't get that far." Before he could mention that his arrival had been the endnote, she added, "It wouldn't have even if you hadn't come home. I was just telling him I couldn't go through with it."

He arched a brow at her. "That sounds pretty convenient."

"It's the truth," she said softly. Something in her voice. He knew she was telling the truth. But he wasn't sure if it made any difference.

God, he was so fucking tired. Had been exhausted since the moment Liv had told him she was pregnant eight years ago. From the first, it'd been so hard, trying to keep up with classes, get a job, and be there for Liv and Matty.

When he'd had to quit school—and hockey—he'd taken solace in the fact that he was doing the right thing for his little family. And that had been enough. It had all been enough.

For a while.

But the sleepless nights, the unbelievably physical demands in the forest, and the pressure not to disappoint Liv wore on him.

He didn't consciously take it out on Liv, and he certainly didn't resent her for becoming pregnant when it was most likely his faulty condom that had put them in the position of being parents so young. And, of course, he wouldn't trade Matty for anything.

And yet, on some level, he knew that a few more kind words to Liv would have pleased her. Taking time while they made love to whisper sweet nothings to her, to tell her how beautiful he thought she was, would have gone a long way.

She never fished for compliments, never begged him to tell her how he felt. What would it have cost him to tell her he loved her? Okay, maybe it wasn't totally true, but couldn't he have just said it anyway? Apparently, she so desperately needed to hear sweet words and feel loved that she went looking elsewhere.

He found he couldn't be angry about it. At least, he couldn't be angry with Liv. They'd both had choices taken away from them when they'd gotten pregnant and decided to marry.

Who knew? Liv might have fallen out of love with Twain a month later and gone away to school or something. She definitely hadn't wanted to carry on tradition and work at the Kitchen. She might have met someone else and had a real courtship filled with dates and flowers. Or become a career woman, finding a niche in some business sector.

Or both.

Whenever he thought about how little it would take to make Liv happy, he'd wrap himself in the nobility of his self-sacrifice. But he wasn't the only one who had given up things to be together for Matty.

"Did it mean anything to you?" he asked.

"No," she said. "Nothing." Again, he believed her. He wouldn't ask why she'd done it—he knew she'd done it for affection. The affection he hadn't given her, though he suspected she wouldn't be able to pinpoint her motive as clearly as he could.

Because he wasn't emotionally involved?

He'd felt anger two nights ago and a burning sting on his pride. But when those two emotions subsided, he realized he felt a weird sense of relief. He didn't want his marriage to end, but there was a part of him that felt just a bit...freer. Free from carrying the burden of Liv's love.

"So," he said, cautiously, not really sure what he wanted the next answer to be, "you have no plans to...be with him?"

Liv looked stunned and recoiled slightly, like he'd hit her or something. "No. God, no. I...I mean...I want to be with you, Twain. I've only ever wanted to be with you."

The relief in her words far outweighed the fleeting sensation of the possibilities of the unknown. "Good," he said. "Then, let's just, I guess, forget the whole thing happened."

He braced himself for her to fling herself in his arms, but she stayed on her side of the table, studying him. "Is that what you want? For us to go on as we were?" Her head tilted, and there was a knowing look in her blue eyes that unsettled him.

"Yes. That's what I want. What do you want?"

"I want…" She clasped her hands in front of her and looked beyond him for a second, thinking. Then she laid her hands flat on the table. "I want a husband, a partner, who loves me." He started to open his mouth, but she interrupted. "Who is *in love* with me."

"Liv, I care very much for you, you know that. I love our family. I love what we have. And I don't think one little mistake should forfeit all we've worked for."

"And it has been work, hasn't it?" she said. No accusation in her voice. Just stating a fact.

"Marriage can be work, yes. Hard work. Especially when you start out young and with a baby like we did. But…"

"But what?" she asked.

He was stumped. And more than a little pissed. How the hell had the tide turned so that he was trying to convince his wife— who had been undressed with a strange man in Twain's bed two nights ago—that he was good enough for her? Why was he the one fighting for their marriage when she was the one so in love with him?

Like he'd said the words out loud, she sat back in her chair with a look of defeat on her face, and shame washed through Twain. In fact, knowing he was hurting Liv now stung him more deeply than walking in on her and that asshat the other night.

And that fact alone sent even more shame and guilt through him.

She leaned forward, taking her hands off the table and placing them in her lap, as if she didn't trust herself not to reach out for him. "Twain, are you in love with me?"

"I care for you so much, Liv. I love our family."

"Are you in love with me? Deep, soul-stirring, can't-live-without-me love?"

He hated to hurt her, but he'd never lied to her, and he couldn't start now. "No," he said.

"Because that's what I feel for you. You know that, right?"

"Yes," he said quietly. He almost couldn't look at her. He felt like a ten-year-old who had broken a toy. In a way, he had broken something. Something very precious.

"I deserve that, you know," she said.

He leaned forward, his arms on the table. "I know you do, Liv. And I'm so, so sorry I can't give it to you. I wish I could."

She nodded, swallowed. "I know you do. Because you're a good man, Twain."

He gave a nervous chuckle. "Christ, Liv, it sounds like you're breaking up with me."

An involuntary laugh came from her, rough and sounding like it hurt her throat. The sound certainly seemed to surprise her. "Ha, can you believe that?" She shook her head and then looked straight at him. "I guess I am."

"No, Liv. You don't mean it. We've just had a shock and we can get—"

She held up a hand and shook her head. "I mean it. Yes, we can get past this. If you can, I easily can, because it meant nothing to me. But it's opened my eyes to something I've been hiding from all these years. Something I can't unsee."

Panic started to rise in him, even though something in her words rang true. Arguments went through his mind. If all else failed, he could take her to bed, and tell her all would be well. He knew he could talk her out of leaving him. She'd been in love with him for ages.

And yet, what would that solve? Where would they be tomorrow? Next week? In two years? Would his feelings change? If they did, would it be enough, or would they circle around and around for years and come to the same conclusion they had tonight?

Finally, he said, "I just want you to be happy, Liv."

She nodded. Tears were welling in her eyes, and he felt them coming on himself. "I know," she said, "and I think I need to concentrate on making myself happy for a change and not making that your responsibility."

"But I…" What? What could he say to that? Nothing. And

so they sat that way for a long time, neither one saying anything. Knowing it was over.

Later, he warned her that people would want an excuse for the abrupt ending to their seemingly happy marriage. "They'll assume I cheated on you," he said.

"But that's not true. I'll tell them—"

"No. Please, Liv. Do this for us. Don't say anything. Let them think whatever they want. Don't give them anything. People will twist it anyway. People will ask. Just say you don't want to talk about it. They won't be satisfied with that, but don't say anything else."

"But there's no way I'm going to let people think you're a cheater when I—"

"As a favor to me, please. Just let them say what they're going to say. Don't try to set the record straight. Don't try to protect me."

"But they'll understand if I explain it. I mean, at least to my family and people like that."

"And say what?" He shook his head. "That, in the end, you being in bed with some guy had no bearing on our marriage breaking up? No one will believe that. Let me save some pride. Don't let people know I was cuckolded."

"That's not why. You couldn't care less if people think I cheated on you. *You're* just trying to protect *me*. You know people will hate me if it got out. To them, I took hockey away from you by getting pregnant, saddled you in a marriage you didn't want, and then I go and cheat—"

"Stop, Liv," he said firmly but gently. "It doesn't matter."

"It's not fair to you," she said.

Maybe not, but it was better this way. The small town would turn on her if they thought she'd cheated on Twain and driven him away. A horrible double standard, but even if people thought that he cheated, he'd fare much better in the public's opinion than she would. And in the end, he owed her something for not being able to love her like she deserved.

"Promise me," he said.

And though she was still shaking her head in disagreement, she whispered, "I promise."

Twenty-Nine

"I'M SORRY I WAS SUCH A JACKASS AT JOE'S PARTY. YOU didn't do anything other than what I asked you to do when we split up," Twain said when he came to her house the next Saturday night after working with Matt all day. They hadn't spoken all week except for a few texts about Matt's schedule. Liv had started to call him a dozen times, but in the end hadn't.

Matty had come in with Twain and headed straight for the shower. He was being allowed to sleep at the Porters' house for the first time since the night he'd messed up so badly, and Twain was going to drop him off on his way home after Matty had washed up.

"It's okay. I'm sure it wasn't fun for you to hear my sisters like that."

He shrugged. "No. But nothing that you probably haven't heard for the past seven years."

It was her turn to shrug. "And you? Did you hear stuff like that a lot?"

He brought himself to his full, staggering height and width. "Not to my face."

She giggled. It felt good to do; she'd been so keyed up the past week.

"Come on in," she said, waving him to the kitchen. "Have you eaten? I think I have some—"

"You don't have to feed me every time I'm here, Liv. I love

your food, but you don't have to wait on me, you know."

"I know." And she did. He'd never expected her to do all the cooking even when they'd been married. She fed Twain because she liked to see him eat her food. And she always made too much anyway. She'd never really learned to cook for just her and Matty. And now with him eating so many of his meals out with friends and with Twain, it seemed like a never-ending cycle of leftovers.

He followed her into the kitchen, but refused all offers of food. "I'll take some coffee, though," he said. "But I can make it. Want some?"

She nodded, sat at the kitchen table, and watched as he made a pot of coffee. He knew where the mugs and sugar were from their week spent together. He even had apparently noticed the mug she favored, bringing it to her, and pouring her a full cup.

He pulled the milk from the fridge and brought it, the sugar bowl, and a filled mug for himself to the table, sitting down across from her.

The scene felt eerily similar to the breakfasts they'd had that week, even though it was seven in the evening. And they hadn't just indulged in mind-blowing sex.

"What time is Matt due at the Porters'?" Twain said, checking his watch.

"I think it was pretty open, but I heard him tell Justin he thought around eight."

"And you're cool with this, right? Giving him a second chance?"

She nodded. "Yes. I'm willing to give him some rope. Hopefully he doesn't hang himself."

He took a drink of coffee. "And let's face it, the Porters are going to watch them like hawks."

"I know. Susan was still so apologetic when she'd called to confirm."

"Better on their watch than ours," Twain said, smiling.

She chuckled. "That's exactly what I was thinking."

"And the other night? You really forgive me for saying what

I did?"

"Of course, Twain. There's nothing to forgive. You only said the truth."

"But you know that's not how I feel, don't you? I mean, I don't think of our marriage as ending because of infidelity."

"I know you don't," she said.

He studied her, and she had to keep from wriggling under his strong gaze. "But do you? Is that what you think?"

She didn't want to go there, had tried not to think about those few days at the end of their marriage ever since her stupid sisters had stirred up memories. "No. Not really."

"Why do you think we split up? After all these years, with the clarity of hindsight, how do you see it happening?"

She'd thought about it a million times over the past seven years, her reasons changing, her ability to see things clearly growing. Lately, about the time she realized that having another child was what she wanted even without a husband, she was able to collect her thoughts and come to a conclusion she could live with.

"I was so afraid of losing you. Always. From the beginning. You must have known that." He nodded, and she continued. "I always felt that I'd gotten you by default. First because you were still on the rebound from Jenny the night of Paula's party, and then because I got pregnant." He started to balk at that, but she held up a hand, wanting to get it all out. "And then I did. Lose you. Even though it was ultimately my doing. And you know what? I lived through it. I was so swamped with guilt for that night with Guthrie and the hurt of what we said two nights later that it took me a while. But then I grew up. Learned to depend on myself, instead of always needing you to define me. And I liked me. I liked who I became. The Liv without Twain.

"I guess you could say that the price I paid to find me was… you," she concluded, taking a deep breath afterward.

"And was it worth it, Liv? Was it worth the price?" There wasn't censure in his voice. He was honestly asking.

She thought about it. Over the years, she'd wished she could take back that day with Guthrie Prince a thousand times. A million. And she still wished that part of it. Being with Guthrie was not the person she was, even then. She had been so lost, so... unformed, that she'd let a little flattery, a little attention and desire turn her head. But that was just it: she *had* let Guthrie turn her head. She'd needed a wake-up call to find out who she was. And she'd needed to know how Twain had really felt about her.

The collateral damage was her marriage.

And, of course, the even bigger collateral damage was divorcing parents for their son, something that brought even more guilt.

In some recess of her mind, Liv felt that even if the afternoon with Guthrie hadn't happened, she and Twain wouldn't have made it. She'd been living with a sense of dread all around her as to when the clock would finally run out on Twain's sense of responsibility to her.

She'd called time before the clock had chimed, but there was no denying their time was running out.

"Yes, it was worth it," she said.

He watched her and then finally nodded. "Good," he said.

"Good? Really?"

He shrugged. "Well, you'd hate for it not to have been worth it."

She tried to smile. "I guess that's true. But it's also pretty selfish on my part."

"Becoming the person you were meant to be, someone stronger, someone you want to be... There's no guilt in wanting that."

"But Matty..."

He waved a hand, then wrapped it around the handle on his mug. "Matt's fine. He's a good kid with a good head on his shoulders."

"And what about you?"

"Me? Hell, I'm tough as nails, Liv. You know that better than anyone."

They sat in silence, sipping their coffee. The shower in Matty's bathroom went off, and she knew she wouldn't have much more time alone with Twain. "What was it you wanted to talk to me about the other night?" At his blank look, she added, "At Joe's party? You came to ask me something, I think you said?"

He looked at her, and she tried to read his face. Indecision. An emotion so rare on Twain Beck she wondered if she imagined it. "It doesn't matter now. I figured out the answer."

"You're sure?" she asked.

"Yeah, I think so." He leaned forward, lowering his voice. "Before Matty comes out, where do we stand with...our project?"

"I took another test this morning, which would have been three weeks. Another negative. So, that's probably a true reading."

"And?"

"And?" she asked with hope in her voice. She'd wondered this week if, after not hearing much from him and the way he'd left Joe's party, Twain would be rescinding his offer of...assistance in her getting pregnant.

"When should we start trying again? When do you think you'll be ovulating again? Or would be a good time to start trying? Or do we just wait now until you get your period and count or something?"

"You're still in?"

"Hell yes. Just let me know when."

"How about right after you drop Matty off at the Porters'?" The timing was probably off, but she found she didn't care.

She heard Matty's bedroom door shut, and in a moment, he was in the kitchen grabbing his jacket, his backpack slung over his shoulder. "Ready, Dad?" he asked Twain.

Twain rose from the table and gave Matty a reminder about the faith they were putting in him by allowing him to return to the scene of the crime and what was expected of him. To Matty's credit, he took Twain's words with a nod and no heavy sighs.

Matty preceded Twain out of the kitchen, and Liv followed

them both to the foyer.

"Thanks for the coffee, Liv," Twain said.

"Thanks for dropping Matty off and saving me a trip," she said.

"*Matt*," Matty said, now conjuring up the exasperated sigh.

"The woman went through seventeen hours of labor giving birth to you. She can call you whatever she wants," Twain said, ruffling Matty's still-wet hair. That he hadn't taken the time to style it reassured Liv that there'd be no midnight raids on Heather Summers' home tonight.

"Liv," Twain said, turning to her. Meeting her eyes, he pointedly said, "I'll see you soon."

"Soon," she confirmed. She watched her men walk out the front door and then returned to the kitchen. After washing out their mugs, she went through to the garage and opened up the door for Twain to park his truck inside.

Then she went to her bedroom and waited.

Thirty

—

"LIV?" TWAIN CALLED, AND SHE DIRECTED HIM BACK TO the bedroom. His big body filled the entire doorway, and she knew that tonight would be different. No more holding back—it hadn't done her any good anyway. She might as well indulge herself.

She was going to look into the face of the man she loved while he held her, kissed her. Created a baby together.

"Hi," she said, almost shyly. Which was silly. They'd had sex in this bed many times during the week Matty was in Florida.

"Hi," he said, entering the room fully. She was sitting up on the bed, leaning against the headboard wearing only a long tee and panties. The comforter was pulled back, sheets crisp and cool on the back of her legs. She waggled a finger at his shirt, and he smiled as he unbuttoned the flannel and threw it on a chair. Then he pulled his thermal over his head, revealing that strong chest and those crazy broad shoulders.

"God, you're beautiful," she said, leaning deeper into her upholstered headboard.

He laughed as he made his way to the bed, undoing his button fly and zipper. "That's my line," he said. He sat on the bed, leaning over the edge to unlace his boots and slide them and his socks off. She scooted up onto her knees and over to him, resting her thighs against his wide back and skimming her hands along his tight muscles. "If the shoe fits…"

Another chuckle as he rose from the bed and turned to face

her. After helping him slide his jeans down his trim hips, she let her hands drift back up as he stepped out of the denim and kicked the pants to the side.

Pulling down the waistband of his boxer-briefs, she freed his erection and took it in her hand, wrapping her fingers around the full girth of him. A soft hiss from him became a louder one as she stroked him twice before leaning over and taking him in her mouth.

"Christ, Liv, that feels so good," he said, his hands tangling in her hair, which she'd left down and loose. It now tumbled over her shoulders in front of her, creating a curtain of privacy. She sucked on him, twirling her tongue, running it hard along the ridge of his head and eliciting another deep groan that she felt in the roof of her mouth.

"Baby, I can't wait," he said, gently tugging on her hair. "I need to be inside you. Now." His tone was more growl than voice, and she felt her insides melt like the ice of the long winter.

Rising up, she felt the moment when he was going to turn her, to make it easier for her not to be face to face. After their talk about not kissing, he had been so good to try to make it as easy as possible for her.

But not tonight. She didn't want easy. She didn't want doggy or spooning or any of the other positions they'd been doing. Not that they weren't all great. And she'd certainly gotten off each time. Multiple times.

As he put his hands on her hips and started to turn her, she wrapped her arms around his neck, rising up on her knees so that her mouth was just below his. Nuzzling his neck, she breathed in the deep pine scent and pressed her breasts against his chest.

Feeling his hand at the base of her t-shirt, she moved away from his body just long enough for him to lift the cotton shirt up and over her head and then toss it to join his jeans on the floor. Once again, she pressed into him, and he hugged her back. The hair on his chest rubbed her nipples, and she moved back and forth as she kissed up his neck, liking the soft abrasion. His hand

214 · MARA JACOBS

slid inside her panties, cupping her bottom, pulling him tight against his hard cock. "Liv," he said in a guttural groan. "Please," he said, trying to turn her again.

"This way," she said, kissing his chin, coming dangerously close to his mouth.

He pulled back. "Liv?" His eyes were questioning and... hopeful.

"Just this once," she whispered. That was all she needed to say. Twain bent the tiny bit needed to fuse his mouth to hers.

Needy at first, hungry. And then he slowed, waiting for her, finding their way together.

He tasted of coffee and the outdoors, though Liv would be hard-pressed to define what the outdoors tasted like. Twain. Always Twain. Their tongues tangled, then he ran his along her lips, as if trying to learn her.

When he'd always known her better than anyone.

He put his hands under her thighs and lifted her from the bed. He came down on the mattress with one knee, laying her down in the center and following her down.

Her panties and his boxer-briefs were off in seconds. She took him in her hand and led him to her. "Wait," he whispered, and her hand stilled. "Kiss me again. Kiss me while you put me inside you."

A tightening in her chest threatened to take over, but she willed herself to nod. She raised her head to kiss him as she opened her thighs wide and cradled his hips, placing him right at her entrance.

He gasped in her mouth as he pushed in, and she raised her hips as she wrapped her arms around his back, wanting him nearer. Deeper. Closer.

Their mouths danced to a silent music that only they heard. As he softly thrust into her, he rose up on his forearms and bracketed her head with his hands on both sides. Leaving her mouth, he placed soft, feather-light kisses all over her face, something she never remembered him doing before.

He traced her jaw line with his tongue and then pulled back to look at her. There was a smoldering, a desire, in his eyes that she hadn't been able to see during the week they'd been having sex in other positions.

Suddenly, she felt more naked, more exposed, than she ever had before. She knew that she couldn't hide her feelings for Twain on her face. She'd never been able to. In years past, she would have whispered that she loved him, and he would bury his head in her neck and kiss her, murmuring words, but never the right ones.

She felt tears welling up in her eyes, and she cursed them. Damn, this was why she hadn't wanted to be face to face. Twain was making her dream of being a mother again a very real possibility. She didn't want to put him in the position of embarrassing him with her tears. With her love.

"Shhh, it's okay," he said. He bent his head, licked a tear from the corner of her eye, and then placed a soft kiss on her eyelid. "It's okay, Liv. It's different this time."

Yes, different. They were adults, not kids. And she should be able to control her heart, her emotions better now.

But she knew that wasn't the case. It would never be the case with Twain.

"Liv, I…" He was staring down at her, concern, or indecision, or something like it, in his eyes. No, she didn't want his pity. Not now. Not when she was looking at his beautiful face, staring into those bright green eyes.

Clenching her inside muscles, she bucked her hips, trying to spur him on. Enough kissing. Enough staring into each other's eyes. Her poor heart could only take so much.

He took the hint, rising up on his haunches, spreading her legs wide, and pushing her thighs up to her chest. But he never took his eyes from hers, even as he pounded into her and the sweat dripped off his forehead.

When he was close, he reached between their joined bodies and circled her clit so that she'd come when he did. Together.

And yet not together in every sense.

He collapsed on the bed, taking her with him as he rolled to the side. She started to find her regular position of her head on his chest, but he dragged her body fully on top of his. "Closer," he said, his voice already drowsy with spent exertion.

Molding her body to his, she kissed him deeply and then buried her head just under his chin. His arms wrapped around her like bands of steel, and she found she liked the feeling.

Liked it too much.

She knew it couldn't happen again. Yes, you couldn't protect your heart, and she'd meant what she'd said to Matty about there being something pure about loving someone so completely, whether they returned the feeling or not.

But she wasn't a masochist, either, and she knew that to continue making love—for that was what she had been doing— with Twain would destroy her.

As she drifted off to sleep, Twain's body under hers, she comforted herself with the thought that at least this time around, she'd known that they were making love for the last time.

Thirty-One

—⁂—

"I DON'T KNOW," TWAIN SAID, MORE TO HIMSELF THAN
to Sawyer, who sat on the stool next to him at Tootie's the next
afternoon. "I think we've worked through it all. I don't think the
past is in our way anymore."

"That's good, right?" Sawyer said, and took a swig from his
beer before setting it back on the smooth wooden bar.

"Yeah, of course."

"So, what's the problem? Sounds like you're right back where
you were a month ago when you decided to have a baby. Only
with less baggage."

"I guess," Twain said, though something wasn't quite right
about Sawyer's assessment. "It's just…" He took a drink of beer,
the ale not going down well, not easing his thoughts in any way.

Nothing eased his thoughts anymore.

Yeah, it was good to have closure with Liv on the past, and
he was glad they'd gotten everything on the table last night. And
then had gotten everything on the bed.

But no, he wasn't right back where he'd started a month ago.
Somewhere during that tumultuous month of making love and
making amends, his feelings for Liv had changed.

It wasn't a bolt of lightning but more a stirring feeling that
had woven itself around him when he hadn't noticed.

When he'd been noticing Liv. The new Liv. The Liv who said
her mind, not waiting to see what Twain wanted. The Liv who ran

her own business and loved every minute of it.

The Liv who didn't fear losing Twain.

And was that it? Was he just some sick fuck who finally wanted his wife when she was finally done wanting him?

No, he didn't think so.

Last night had been amazing. Finally being face to face with her, the emotions had nearly undone him. Tasting her mouth, looking into her eyes as he moved within her. He'd loved every minute of it.

Loved Liv. Was *in love* with her. Loved her so much that it almost pained him to look at her last night and not say anything.

He'd wanted to tell her then, but thought it might mean more if they weren't in bed. And then afterward, she'd pulled away from him. She'd tried to hide it, and had still slept in his arms, but he knew her well enough to know that she was protecting herself.

He couldn't blame her, really.

The other thing was, and it was obvious from their talk, that she didn't *need* him anymore. And like the relief he'd felt when he'd walked in on her and that Scottish jackass, Twain reveled in that fact.

Want was much better than need, in his book.

So was love. And now that Twain was finally able to admit his feelings to himself, everything should fall into place. Right?

"'It's just' what?" Sawyer asked, pulling Twain from his thoughts.

"It's not the same as it was a month ago," he said, looking at his older brother who—damn it—had a smirk of amusement on his face. "You knew?" Twain asked.

"What? That you'd fallen in love with your wife? I suspected."

"Why didn't you say anything?" Twain knew he sounded like a whiny ten-year-old accusing his older brother of keeping a shiny new ball just out of his reach.

And that was kind of what his feelings for Liv felt like—a shiny new ball. But one he already knew how to play with.

Knew how to play with *very* well.

"Wasn't my place," Sawyer said. "Although…"

"Yeah?" Twain said, fully turning himself on the barstool to face Sawyer, who still—maddeningly!—kept facing toward the mirror behind the bar.

"If you hadn't realized it soon, or if it looked like you were going to fuck it up? I would have jumped in."

"Seriously? You had it that thought out?"

He shrugged. "You knocked some sense into me when I was flaking out on Deni. I owed you one."

"Owed me a 'Get your head out of your ass' conversation?"

"Something like that. Though as I recall, there was some shoving into a wall. I was *really* looking forward to that."

"Dick," Twain said, but smiled as he took a drink.

"I can be, yes," Sawyer responded, with a smile of his own.

After a moment of silence and a wave to Linda for new bottles of beer, Twain said, "So, what do I do now? I'm in love with her, and I think she still loves me—"

"Liv will love you until the day you die, you undeserving little shit."

He guffawed at Sawyer's comment of "little." Twain had a couple of inches on his brother and about fifteen pounds of muscle from logging. And that was saying something, because Sawyer was no slouch in the physical department.

"She may still love me, but she doesn't need me."

Sawyer snorted at that. "Like they ever *need* us."

"True." He took a swig of beer. "And I can't jerk her around just because I've finally fallen in love for the first time in my life. I can't do that to her. I'm either in for good or not at all. I can't tell her I love her and then not commit."

"Do you want to commit?"

He didn't hesitate. "Hell yes."

Sawyer nodded. "There you go, then."

"But, even with all that, and even if she loves me, she said from the get-go when we were talking about the baby that she didn't want to get back together."

Sawyer turned from facing forward and looked squarely at Twain. In some ways, it was like looking into a mirror: the same green eyes, the same somewhat cynical weariness.

"Are you telling me you haven't done *anything* in the last month to persuade her that she'd like to have you around full-time?"

Flashes of her clinging to him, the look in her eyes as she called out his name, their limbs entangled as they lay, exhausted, on her bed, scampered through his brain.

"Well...maybe she is more amenable to the idea now than she was a month ago."

"Atta boy."

"But still, how—"

"Jesus, do I have to do everything for you? Tie your shoes for you like I did when you were six?"

"That was Huck."

Sawyer flicked a hand. "Whatever. Tell her you love her, and you want to try again."

The words, so simple, so easy to hear, shot a knife of terror through Twain's gut.

He'd never in his life said "I love you" to a woman.

"And, if you're too chickenshit to say that..." Sawyer said, throwing him a much-needed life vest. Twain suspected that he might indeed be too chickenshit to say the words to Liv without a guarantee of how she felt. "...then *show* her somehow."

"Show her?"

"Yeah, show her."

A sneaking suspicion blossomed in Twain's head. "So, chickenshit, how did you show Deni?"

Sawyer laughed, and Twain joined him, the other patrons at the bar looking their way. One old goat even raised his glass in a toast to the brothers' mirth.

"I *did* tell her I loved her."

"But..."

"But I made her some picture frames and hung them for

her."

"Picture frames? And handyman jobs? That did it?"

Sawyer faced forward again, a private smile on his face, and Twain knew he wouldn't pry any deeper. This was Deni and Sawyer's story. "Let's just say, the frames were…special frames, and it all meant something to her."

"That's good that it worked out for you, but I made Liv tons of stuff when we were married, so there wouldn't be any novelty in that."

Sawyer just took a sip of his beer, keeping quiet while Twain thought.

"I'd been thinking about finishing the basement of the house. For an office and workroom for her."

Sawyer waved a hand. "Too impersonal."

While Twain racked his brain, his brother threw some cash on the bar and rose to leave. "You're leaving now?" Twain asked. "But I don't know what to do."

Sawyer laid a rough hand on Twain's shoulder, just like he had when he'd broken the news to a fourteen-year-old Twain that their father was leaving them. "We've got this," he'd said back then as Twain had tried not to cry in front of his big brother in order to hold it together for Huck, who had been only seven at the time.

"You've got this," Sawyer said to Twain now.

He walked out of the bar, and Twain sat staring at his big brother's back and hoping—praying!—that his words would be true.

Thirty-Two

—m—

"I THINK THAT MAYBE WE SHOULD LOOK AT OTHER options. If the other night didn't work, and I'm not pregnant," Liv said. They were at Twain's house, sitting in his living room. She'd called and asked if she could come over, since she'd be in Calumet to have dinner with her parents. Matty was at her home in Houghton, studying for an algebra test.

He had ushered her into his home and waved her to the big, comfy couch. Now he sat across from her in an oversized chair that fit his big frame to a tee. Leaning forward, forearms on his knees, hands dangling, he said, "It's too soon to know, right? That was only a week ago. But you haven't had your period yet, right?"

"Right."

"Does this have something to do with you just having had dinner at your parents?"

"No," she said.

"You still haven't told them that we're trying?"

"No." Thankfully, her parents had been so busy telling her about their winter in Florida that they hadn't realized Liv was preoccupied with the thoughts that hadn't left her since she and Twain had made love last Saturday night. Her certainty that she couldn't keep making love with Twain. Not even for a baby.

"Oh, okay. Well, I'm glad you stopped by. There's…um… something I want to talk to you about."

Had he felt it too? Was he also trying to end their physical relationship? That night he'd been so tender, so sweet, but Liv didn't want his pity.

"Wait. What did you say first? That you wanted to try a different option?"

"Right," she said, trying to make herself comfortable on the couch. She pulled up her legs, tucking them under, but that didn't feel right. She stayed where she was, though, trying to convey a casual air about her, even though she felt anything but casual. How could she, when she was discussing her heart?

A heart she'd protected for so long, which was now at risk of shattering forever.

"I was thinking that if the other night didn't work, that maybe we should try something different."

Confusion crossed his handsome face. "Like…with a pillow under you or something? Keeping your legs in the air after? Liv, I know we're a lot older than when we so effortlessly got pregnant with Matty, but we haven't really given it a good shot yet. I mean, there was that week. And then last Saturday. That's it. It might just take time."

"No, that's not what I meant. I mean, like…looking at artificial insemination."

More confusion. "Don't you think we should give it a couple of months trying naturally?"

She uncurled her legs—no sense trying to fake it anymore. Time to lay it on the line. "It's not that. I'm not thinking AI to better our chances, though it probably would."

"And cost a lot of money."

"I have some put aside for it, if needed."

He waved her words aside. "Money you could use when the baby comes, or for college or whatever." His arms came off his knees, straightening; he knew now that something in her had changed, shifted. "If it's not to better our chances, then…"

"I can't…have sex with you anymore."

"Can't or won't?"

"Won't, I suppose. Would rather not."

His body went on alert, shoulders back, chest out, like some caveman smelling a threat. "Is there someone else? Are you back with Kevin Schmidt?" There was something in his voice that hadn't been there seven years ago when he'd asked her the same questions about Guthrie Prince. Yes, something very different about his posture, his voice, his facial expression of...was that jealousy? Surely not.

"No, nobody else. Certainly not Kevin. It has nothing to do with anybody other than...me, really."

"Not even me? This doesn't even include me?"

A calmness came over her. "No, not really. This is about me doing what I need."

"Like when you asked me to leave seven years ago?"

Was it really any different? She was saving herself then, too. "I guess so, yes."

He rose from the chair, his big body uncoiling. Running a hand through his dark hair, he looked at the ceiling. "I don't believe this." He turned to her. "You're breaking up with me?"

"Well, I don't think you could really say—"

"We were together. At least that last time. It might have been private, it might have been for a specific reason, but don't insult my intelligence. We were very much *together*."

"You're right," she admitted, not wanting to quibble over semantics.

"So you are? Calling whatever we have together off?"

"Yes," she said.

He started laughing. Laughing! Her heart was being torn apart making this decision, and he was laughing at her?

"I'm sorry," he said, holding a hand out to stop her as she started to rise from the couch. "I'm sorry. I don't mean to laugh. Please, sit."

"I know it doesn't mean that much to you," she said, "but this was really hard—"

"That's why I'm laughing," he said. "Because it *does* mean that much to me. Finally. And I'm just about to lose you. Again."

She shook her head, trying to make sense of his words. "Wait," he said. "Before you say anything else, let me just ask you one question. And don't even speak, just nod or shake yes or no, okay?"

She nodded, eyeing him warily. It wasn't like Twain to play games, especially not with her emotions. He'd been so good when they'd been married to never exploit the fact that she was helplessly in love with him, and he…well, he just wasn't.

"Is the reason that you're saying all of this because you still love me and you're afraid you'll be hurt?"

Nod.

"Okay. Good." He laughed at her frown. "Not good, that's not what I— Holy wah, I'm mucking this up, but good, eh?"

Not knowing what "this" was, she only shrugged.

"I…we…ah, shit." He placed his hands on his hips, looking down at her, frustration clearly on his face. Then he looked behind him, out the window to the backyard, and she could tell that inspiration had struck. "Come on," he said, taking her hand and pulling her up from the couch.

He led her through the kitchen and out the back door, nearly dragging her down the few steps and across his back lawn to a large pole barn. "In here," he said, opening the door and stepping back for her to pass.

When he flicked on the light behind her, she saw that she was in what was part equipment storage and part woodworking shop. She knew he did some woodworking at the T&B offices, but from the looks of it, he had an elaborate setup here as well.

"This is what I want to show you," he said, still holding her hand as he brought her into the corner of the large building where a lathe, sander, and other equipment sat. On top of one of the tables was an exquisite piece of wood about three feet long and two feet high. When she got closer, the pattern of striations and grains took her breath away. She also saw that the piece had been hollowed out and was like a large, oval bowl. Except it had rocking feet, or what looked like was going to become rocking feet.

"Is this…are you creating a…"

"Bassinet? Yes." He ran his hand along the top of the beautiful maple. "There's still a lot of shaping to do, and carving, but it'll be ready for the baby."

She examined the little cradle-to-be, tracing twists and turns of the different grains. "This came from a burl, right?"

"Yes," he said. She could hear the pride in his voice as he stood behind her.

"The one you and Matty harvested a couple of weeks ago?"

"Yep."

"I thought he said you were going to use that for a bar for Petey Ryan or something? He was all excited about it."

He laid a large hand on her shoulder, and she fought the urge to lean back into him. The bassinet was beautiful, but it didn't change why she'd come here tonight. "I'll find something else for Petey's bar. I'll do it pro bono, even. I wanted this piece for our baby. For our future."

She turned, his hand staying on her shoulder. Twisting away from him, she stepped aside. "It's beautiful Twain. Thank you. I…I can't wait to place our child in it." She cleared her throat, trying to quell the rising emotions in her.

She'd come here because she knew it was the right thing to do. She'd known it seven years ago—she was not the kind of person who could love and not be loved in return.

"So?" he said, with what seemed to be expectation on his face.

"So…thanks again for showing me. It's going to be spectacular."

"But wait," he said, when she made a move to leave the pole barn. He looked from her to the bassinet and back again. "Don't you see?"

"No, what?"

He pointed to the piece of wood. "That. That's to show you that…" He ran his hand through his hair again, and over his beard (four days of growth, if she were to guess). "Christ, Sawyer's such an asshole."

"What does Sawyer— Twain, why did you want to show me this? Why are you building the bassinet?"

He shrugged, then sighed. "Apparently that's what we Beck boys do to win back the women we love…we build them things. Sawyer made Deni picture frames, I made you this bassinet."

"Well, that's nice, but…"

"I knew it wouldn't work. Sawyer seemed to think that—"

"Wait. Love?"

Now she had his attention. "Yes, love," he said, with a tone like "What did you think we were talking about?"

Men.

"Twain. Forget the bassinet. Forget what Sawyer built Deni." He looked at the cradle like it held his next lines, but wasn't coughing them up. She took his hands in hers and looked up at him until his eyes moved from the wood to her. "Twain, what are you trying to say?"

"Love. I'm in love with you. And I want us to try again. And not just for the baby."

Hope bloomed in her heart, so big and strong that whatever pebbles of her Pet Rock that might have remained were ground to dust.

As she did seven years ago, she asked, "Are you in love with me? Deep, soul-stirring, can't-live-without-me love?"

His answer this time was different than that of seven years ago. With no hesitation whatsoever, and a huge grin, he said, "Yes. Yes, I am. I am hopelessly, completely, head-over-heels in love with you, Liv Koskela Beck."

He bent down and took her mouth with his, kissing her with a tenderness, and a love, she'd never in her life experienced. Twining her arms around his neck, she kissed him back, tears streaming down her face. Or maybe the tears were his, she couldn't tell.

They kissed for what seemed like forever, though when he finally pulled back and looked down at her with the love he felt so evident in his gaze, Liv knew that even forever wouldn't be long

228 ☙   MARA JACOBS

enough.

She had paid the ultimate price seven years ago to become the woman Twain now loved. And she knew...it had been worth it.

~*~

Author's Note

A huge thank you to Cindy Cowell for her insights and information on the life of a logger. And, for what it's like to love a logger. Also, thanks to Amy Pellizzaro for additional logging information, and for turning me on to tree burls. I became a little obsessed with some of the gorgeous bowls I found online during my research.

Beta readers Holli Bertram, Liz Kelly and Patti Kearly were invaluable in their feedback. The editing at Word Wolfe and Editing 720 was, as always, top notch. And a big thank you to my last-look editor, Margo Burrage.

The Worth Series continues with

WORTH THE LIES
THE WORTH SERIES BOOK 6
HUCK BECK'S STORY

—✺—

WORTH THE FLIGHT
THE WORTH SERIES BOOK 7

Or try Mara's New Adult Romance Series

IN TOO DEEP
FRESHMAN ROOMMATES TRILOGY, BOOK 1

IN TOO FAST
FRESHMAN ROOMMATES TRILOGY, BOOK 2

IN TOO HARD
FRESHMAN ROOMMATES TRILOGY, BOOK 3

—✺—

Mara Jacobs is the *New York Times* and *USA Today* bestselling author of The Worth Series

After graduating from Michigan State University with a degree in advertising, Mara spent several years working at daily newspapers in advertising sales and production. This certainly prepared her for the world of deadlines!

She writes mysteries with romance, thrillers with romance, and romances with…well, you get it.

Forever a Yooper (someone who hails from Michigan's glorious Upper Peninsula), Mara now splits her time between the Copper Country, Las Vegas, and East Lansing, where she is better able to root on her beloved Spartans.

You can find out more about Mara's books at
www.marajacobs.com

Mara loves to hear from readers. Contact her at
mara@marajacobs.com

www.ingramcontent.com/pod-product-compliance
Lightning Source LLC
Chambersburg PA
CBHW031723170626
46808CB00005B/1870